SMUT

SMUT

Two Unseemly Stories

Alan Bennett

This edition first published
in 2011 by Faber and Faber Ltd
Large Print edition published 2012
by AudioGO Ltd
by arrangement with
Faber and Faber Ltd

Hardcover ISBN: 978 1 445 89268 9
Softcover ISBN: 978 1 445 89269 6

British Library Cataloguing in Publication Data available

Printed and bound in Great Britain by
MPG Books Group Limited

CONTENTS

THE GREENING OF
MRS DONALDSON

'I gather you're my wife,' said the man in the waiting room. 'I don't think I've had the pleasure. Might one know your name?'

Middle-aged and scrawny, he was bare-legged and underneath his shortie dressing gown Mrs Donaldson thought he might be bare altogether.

'Donaldson.'

'Right. Mine's Terry. I've been away.'

He put out his hand and as she shook it briefly the dressing gown fell open to reveal a pair of tangerine Y-fronts with, tucked into the waistband, a mobile phone.

'Trouble in the back passage,' he said cheerfully.

'No,' said Mrs Donaldson. 'I don't think so.'

'Mine not yours, dear,' said Terry. 'You're just my wife.'

'I was given to understand,' said Mrs Donaldson, 'that it was your waterworks.'

'No fear.' Terry hitched up his Y-fronts. 'No way.'

'Frequency,' said Mrs Donaldson. 'Waking at night.'

'Absolutely not. I go before I come to bed and then first thing in a morning. Well, you know that,' and he sniggered. 'You're my wife.'

Mrs Donaldson took out a folder.

'I think you'll find,' said Terry, 'it's the other department. Stools hard and difficult to pass. Occasional blood. All that. I thought I could be very shy, which is why you're here: to hold my hand.'

'Well I was a nurse,' admitted Mrs Donaldson. 'I'm au fait with all the technical terms . . . bowel,

3

colon, prostate.'

'Steady on,' said Terry. 'Were you a nurse?'

'No,' said Mrs Donaldson. 'I'm a widow.'

'Hold on a sec,' said Terry. 'I'll go and ascertain,' and fastening his dressing gown he left the room.

When he came back he found her sitting in a different seat. He sat down next to her again but without speaking.

'And?' said Mrs Donaldson.

Terry indicated his crotch. 'Waterworks it is, though the bowel could come into it apparently as they'll have to go in the back door first to size up the old prostate. After that it depends on how much he wants to throw at them.'

The door opened. There was the sound of laughter and a girl with a name tag came out in tears.

'I did try and tell you dear,' said an elderly woman who followed, buttoning her blouse. 'The gall bladder was just a red herring.'

A buzzer went. Terry and Mrs Donaldson got up.

'After you,' said Terry, putting a single finger in the small of Mrs Donaldson's back. She wriggled it off, saying, 'You're shy, remember?'

There were half a dozen students this morning, four boys, two girls, with the place roughly rigged out to represent a consulting room. There was a desk, a table and, lounging at the back in seeming indifference, Dr Ballantyne, the head of the unit. Who was Terry again? Mrs Donaldson thought, though doubtless in superior underpants.

'Good morning, Mrs Donaldson, Mr Porter.' Ballantyne uncoiled from his chair.

'I won't say, "How are you?" because that's for our budding healers to find out, though I'm afraid

4

we are minus Miss Truscott who has retired hurt. Well come along, come along. Isn't somebody going to ask these good people to sit down?' He sat down himself. 'Mr Rowswell, you're in charge.'

A nervous red-faced boy with odd ears and whose jacket was too big for him got them awkwardly sat down and took his unaccustomed seat behind the desk.

Searching for his hand up his sleeve he looked at Terry and attempted a smile.

'What seems to be the trouble?'

Ballantyne sighed heavily and put his hands on his head.

'Congratulations, Mr Rowswell. You are only in your second year of medical studies yet you are already possessed of a skill that has not been vouchsafed to me in twenty years of practice. You can tell who is sick and who is not.'

The class obligingly tittered.

'How do you know which of these two seemingly healthy people is the patient?'

Rowswell blushed.

'He's in his dressing gown.'

Ballantyne looked at Terry as if seeing him for the first time.

'So he is. Why is that, Mr Porter?'

Terry rubbed his bare knees.

'I thought it would save time.'

'We are not here to save time, Mr Porter. We are here—' and he smiled graciously at Mrs Donaldson, 'to save lives. In the future do not jump the gun.

'Supposing Mrs Donaldson were the patient, I would not expect her to present herself . . .' he considered briefly, 'in her negligee.'

With a kindly smile he let the thought linger a

5

moment. 'Proceed, Mr Rowswell.'

Mrs Donaldson had been coming to the medical school for a month or so now and to the hospital itself for much longer. It was here that Mr Donaldson had slowly and not unpainfully died, visited daily by his uncomplaining wife in a routine she had begun by finding irksome but to which she had grown inured and even attached so that his eventual death came as a double deprivation; she missed the visiting as much as the visited and in the afternoons particularly was now somewhat at a loss. With no compelling reason to go out she stayed at home for weeks on end, a process Gwen, her married daughter, was pleased to dignify as 'grieving' and was rather gratified by, never having felt her mother gave her father his due.

Though her husband had been an unobjectionable man and Mrs Donaldson genuinely regretted his passing, she did not feel nevertheless that she was quite ready to school herself for the dignified solitude her daughter thought was appropriate to her widowed status. Deliverance came from an unexpected quarter.

A muddle over her husband's pension had left his widow less well-provided-for than had been foreseen and so needing to supplement her income. Now alone in a three-bedroomed house it occurred to her that she might take in some students.

While her daughter could not dispute the economic sense of this proposal she found its social implications distasteful.

'Lodgers? In Lawnswood? I don't think Daddy would like that. And I don't see you as a landlady.'

'Renting the odd room doesn't make me a landlady. Besides,' said Mrs Donaldson, 'they're not

6

lodgers, they're students.'

Gwen didn't argue, reasoning that a few months of tidemarks in the bath, late-night music and unflushed toilets would make the point forcibly enough.

'The first condom in the loo,' she said to her husband, 'and she'll soon change her tune.'

It may be that Mrs Donaldson was lucky but the two students sent to her by the university lodgings syndicate were in every respect but one not to be faulted. They were neat, quiet and they cleaned the bath and flushed the toilet and were so altogether discreet Mrs Donaldson scarcely knew they were in the house. Laura was a medical student and Andy, her boyfriend, was doing architecture (Mrs Donaldson thought this might have something to do with their neatness), and it was through them that Mrs Donaldson had been taken on as a part-time demonstrator, the advert spotted by Laura in the medical-school bulletin.

No special skills were said to be required, only the ability to memorise information and present it clearly. Nothing was said in the advert about acting ability or Mrs Donaldson would not have applied; self-confidence wasn't mentioned either, which would have been another deterrent as Mrs Donaldson had always thought of herself as shy.

It was a point not lost on Gwen to whom she was unwise enough to mention her application.

'For a start you don't like taking your clothes off.'

'I don't,' agreed her mother, 'but it's in a good cause.'

'I'd have thought you'd have seen enough of hospitals. I don't know what Daddy would think'—

7

Gwen's role, as Mrs Donaldson often felt, her father's representative on earth.

Respectable and even praiseworthy though the job was, her daughter saw it as neither; what her mother was planning to do making her a distant relation of the artist's model with some of the brazenness and even nudity that that occupation could involve.

In fact Mrs Donaldson had never been required to remove her clothing, which some patients were more 'into' than others, Terry for instance never slow to get into a hospital gown even when his particular animated diagnostic conundrum scarcely required it.

Mrs Donaldson felt that such readiness to disrobe was practically a symptom in itself, though of what she would have found it hard to say, sadness just about covering it and also middle age. But it was an inclination she was happy not to share.

'I don't even see it as acting,' she told her friend Delia in the canteen, 'just a case of keeping a straight face. It's a way of not being yourself.'

Delia was another member of the medical troupe.

'It's just nice to be looked at,' said Delia, 'even as a specimen. How often do young people ever look at you? At our age we're invisible.'

Though their paths only occasionally crossed and few people at the hospital knew of their extramural association it happened this morning that Laura was in the class where Mrs Donaldson was demonstrating and indeed had now taken over the examination of Terry from the blushing Mr Rowswell who, about to conduct a rectal

8

examination, had fallen at the first fence.

'Gently, gently,' said Dr Ballantyne. 'Think of it as your girlfriend.'

For Mr Rowswell who had never had a girlfriend this was no help but Laura was now doing rather better, so much so that Ballantyne felt able to slip outside to take a call on his mobile.

It was at this point that Mrs Donaldson suddenly pitched forward on the table unconscious.

All eyes being on Terry it was a moment or two before anybody even noticed. Then they all crowded round, someone opening a vacant glassy eye and one of the girls (not Laura) fumbling with Mrs Donaldson's dress to try and locate the heart.

'I'll get somebody,' said Terry, who had rapidly pulled up his pants and got on his mobile. 'Who do you ring?'

'Fuck me,' said Rowswell. 'This one's got piles and the other one's had a stroke.'

'Or has she?' said Minskip. 'It might be all part of the act.'

'No,' said Terry. 'I'd know if it were. She was just supposed to be my wife.'

'In any case,' said Rowswell, 'we haven't done strokes.'

Now Dr Ballantyne returns and all doubt as to the gravity of the situation is banished. Sizing up the contingency immediately he gets on his mobile to summon the resuscitation unit. Then, never one to let an opportunity slip, in the interval before it arrives takes the students through the procedures consequent on what is plainly some sort of cerebral accident.

'Could it be stress?' said Terry. 'She was quite chippy with me earlier on. Only she looks the type

who keeps it under.'

Ballantyne ignores this, simply saying, 'Where the fuck are they? Time is of the essence. We're in a hospital already. What would happen if she was out on the street?'

'Mrs Donaldson,' said Laura, kneeling by the unconscious woman. 'Mrs Donaldson.' And, tearfully, 'I know her, you see. She's my landlady.'

'Is there anything else we could possibly be doing?' said Ballantyne. 'Think, you idiots. Think!'

Everybody thought, knowing, though, that if there was anything else to be done Dr Ballantyne would have done it. 'She has a daughter,' Laura said. 'Perhaps we should try and get hold of her.' Mrs Donaldson's frock had ridden up her legs, revealing stocking tops secured by suspenders, a form of fastening so archaic it was only the gravity of the situation that stopped Ballantyne drawing it to the students' attention. As it was he gently eased the frock down, lifting Mrs Donaldson's legs in the process and saying kindly to the insensible form, 'There we are.'

Laura was still knelt beside her and now put her hand on her neck.

'Her pulse is good.'

'Yes,' said Dr Ballantyne, 'only you're taking it in a glove that has just been up Mr Porter's bottom.'

The insensible woman gave a perceptible start.

'She's coming round,' said Terry.

'That's because she's never been away,' said Ballantyne.

'All over, dear lady. You can get up now.' And he helped Mrs Donaldson back onto her chair.

'Ballantyne obviously fancies you,' said Delia when they were talking in the canteen afterwards.

And when Mrs Donaldson pulled a face, 'You could do a lot worse.'

There had been some chuntering after Mrs Donaldson had 'come round'.

While all the students were in varying degrees abashed, the most put out was Terry, who, seeing himself as virtually a paramedic, felt entitled as one of the group to be in on the subterfuge. But, as Mrs Donaldson knew but did not like to admit to herself, this was unlikely to happen if only because she was a fragrant fifty-five-year-old widow with neat shapely legs whereas Terry was an unbecoming long-nosed scruffy-looking man with lank, sagging underpants and a tattoo of a bluebird startled out of his navel.

Still Terry was right; they were a group, if an ill-assorted one. With no qualification required and with its skills undefined it was hardly surprising that the troupe was recruited from the dropouts of a variety of other occupations. Typical was Delia, who had been an actress and would still describe herself as such; Terry had been (among other things) a security guard and a hospital porter; what Miss Beckinsale had done nobody knew but as the oldest it enabled her to be both superior and condescending and with a claim, too, to specialised medical knowledge having once briefly worked in a chemist's.

Into this ramshackle assemblage Mrs Donaldson didn't fit at all. She was (or thought herself) a conventional middle-class woman beached on the shores of widowhood after a marriage that had been, she supposed, much like many others . . . happy to begin with, then satisfactory and finally dull. But thinking herself typical, in this motley

11

company she was anything but.

It meant, though, that she had to put on two performances. In herself she had to seem more open-minded, more 'relaxed' than she sometimes felt, lest she seem prim.

'I've never even liked swearing,' she confessed to Delia, 'so when people swear I feel out of it.'

'Don't worry,' said Delia. 'Two months of this place and you'll be saying "shit" with the best of them.' (She actually meant 'fuck' but didn't think Mrs Donaldson was quite ready for this yet.)

Her other performance was as one of the group when she had, like the rest of them, to pretend to be whatever the case notes required . . . a grieving mother, a depressed daughter, a truculent patient. On the whole this second line of pretence came easier to her than the first. The job involved some degree of preparation with the SPs, or Simulated Patients as they were officially designated, required to familiarise themselves with the circumstances of the person they would be representing and which, apart from the particular symptoms being presented or the predicament to be explored, included social background and medical history. This meant that last thing at night she was often reading up the case notes for the next day. That she was more conscientious about this than some of the others Dr Ballantyne was not slow to notice, with the result that she was given some demanding situations and the more rarefied conditions. She was, there was no doubt about it, an asset.

Still, conscientious though she was, she felt badly that she had been unable to tip Laura the wink about her upcoming falling down but Ballantyne had only cleared it with her shortly before the class

12

began, treating it as some sort of trick he wanted to play on the students rather than as a proper teaching exercise. Mrs Donaldson hadn't cared for the sense of conspiracy in which Ballantyne had cloaked the manoeuvre ('Our little secret'), preferring always to know well in advance what it was she was supposed to be suffering from so that she could have all the symptoms at her fingertips. True, this pretend cerebral accident only involved her passing out but were there other warning signs . . . a headache for instance, which she could have referred to beforehand or more plainly counterfeited? Ballantyne brushed these considerations aside, even giving her a squeeze of congratulations afterwards, so that as with some of his other antics she felt the whole thing had less to do with the enlightenment of the students than with getting on a more intimate footing with her . . . something he had not yet managed to do.

'You can understand it,' said Delia. 'You've lost your husband, he's lost his wife. A son in Botswana apparently and the daughter's married an optician. He's probably lonely.'

When Mrs Donaldson got home Laura was in the kitchen.

'To tell you the truth,' said Laura, 'I felt a bit sorry for you. He's so disgusting.'

'Terry?' said Mrs Donaldson. 'Yes, he is.'

'No . . . or rather yes but Terry's just a creep. I meant Ballantyne. All that, "You can get up now, dear lady."' She pulled a face. 'I'm surprised you go along with it. Don't you ever get embarrassed?'

'He's a man,' said Mrs Donaldson. 'And I only had to faint. Besides I should be grateful; the money comes in so useful.'

13

This was not an unconsidered remark.

Ideal though the young people were, in one respect (and that not the least important) they were both a disappointment and a worry since they were regularly behind with the rent. It did no harm, Mrs Donaldson thought, occasionally to remind them that householder though she was and with her own little car she was not exactly flush and that their contribution to the housekeeping, if and when they chose to make it, was not just a bonus; it was essential.

Had her daughter been made aware of the young people's payment record Mrs Donaldson would never have heard the end of it, and so contentious an area was it she had the sense to keep it to herself, never in this or any other respect expressing less than satisfaction with what Gwen still referred to as 'the lodgers'.

To be fair, the children, as Mrs Donaldson thought of them, were not unconcerned about their own fecklessness. They did not want to be reported to the lodgings syndicate still less thrown out and Laura had made up her mind to speak to Mrs Donaldson just at the time Mrs Donaldson had determined to speak to her.

Laura got in first taking the older woman's hand.

'About the rent,' she said.

'Yes?' said Mrs Donaldson.

'What's this, what's this?' said Andy coming into the kitchen. 'Holding hands?'

'I was just telling Mrs D. We'll get there in the end. With the rent.'

Andy took her other hand.

'Yes. We'll work something out.'

Mrs Donaldson didn't think there was much to

14

work out. They owed her money. It ought to be paid.

But Laura had made her a cup of tea and Andy volunteered to change the Hoover bag so the moment passed.

Mrs Donaldson's next session at the medical school was with a duodenal ulcer, a complaint which she had no need to read up on as Mr Donaldson had suffered from it for most of his adult life. She knew all the symptoms, the site of the pain and what brought it on, which, in the case she was presenting, she decided was stress from her job as personal assistant to a captain of industry. What had brought it on with Mr Donaldson she couldn't think; herself, she wondered sometimes, but if so he had never let on.

These were the first year and the diagnosis involved some inexpert kneading of her diaphragm, the students so vigorous in their application that Mrs Donaldson's cry of pain when they hit the spot was scarcely feigned at all.

Ordinarily Dr Ballantyne would have been quick to protect the proto-patients against overzealous interference by the students if only because it was almost a ritual opportunity for heavy sarcasm ('Has difficulty in swallowing, Mr Horrocks? Hardly surprising when you've got your fist down his throat'). Today, though, it was different as he was wholly taken up with a new weapon in the clinical armoury, a camcorder with which he was recording the proceedings.

Ballantyne insisted on wielding it personally ('It's a therapeutic tool. One needs to know where to point it. A camera to me is like a knife to a surgeon'). That he often pointed it at her

15

notwithstanding, Mrs Donaldson thought it more of a toy than a tool but this was because her husband had been prey to similar passing technological fancies which were equally jealously guarded. The lawnmower had been a proscribed area, the CD player and even the electric carving-knife, all of which his death had liberated for her promiscuous deployment, one of the several joys of bereavement being that she no longer had to play the little woman.

Mrs Donaldson was also sceptical of the filming process itself since she felt the camera brought out the worst in the Simulated Patients, tempting them to dramatise and show off, an assessment with which Delia tended to agree.

'How can you be natural with that thing poking up your nose?'

There was Terry, for instance, who that afternoon had been diagnosed with terminal cancer. Now whenever he felt the camera in the offing he looked into the middle distance as if contemplating his tragic future and the coming beyond.

Miss Beckinsale, though never one to underplay, was in this instance unimpressed. As she pointed out to Mrs Donaldson she was no stranger to the camera, as her presentation of dementia was so highly thought of she had even done it 'on a proper camera' in Glasgow and taken it to a case conference in the Isle of Man.

As it was, Mrs Donaldson's scepticism over the camcorder seemed fully justified. The following Thursday she had Crohn's Disease but by this time the instrument had lost much of its appeal and seemed no longer to be the vital weapon in the fight

16

against disease it had been the week before.

To be fair, this was not due to Ballantyne's lightmindedness. He thought highly of his little troupe who were in their way pioneers. But when he came to review the material he had shot Ballantyne was depressed to find how unconvincing so much of it seemed; it was lengthy, flat and wholly without form. Presentations which at the time he had found real and natural, on tape seemed stagey and contrived.

Some of this could be put down to the inexperience of the patient simulators where the camera was concerned but in fact all that was wrong was that the tape needed editing. With nobody to put him right Ballantyne gave up on the whole experiment and since he could scarcely explain or account for this to the group it seemed to confirm Mrs Donaldson's unkind presentiment at the start.

She at least had come over well on tape, or so the doctor thought, while at the same time aware that he looked on her with a kindlier eye than he did on any of her colleagues; if the truth were known he was also slightly afraid of her. Had she been aware of this she in her turn might have felt kindlier towards the doctor, but, as it was, all she and Delia saw was that the toy of the week before now spent much of the session confined to the top of its tripod where it surveyed what went on with its single Cyclopean eye.

'And then they say they're underfunded,' said Delia.

At home the matter of the rent remained unresolved with the young people now four weeks in arrears. Cyril would never have put up with it, she told herself, though he would never have had

17

lodgers in the first place and her own resentment made her feel both a bore and a spoilsport. Still she determined to speak out.

Actually she hadn't seen them for several days, both keeping out of her way she imagined, but coming in from the hospital one evening she found them together in the kitchen and it was as if they had been waiting for her.

Andy made her a cup of tea. (That was the way they were good, she thought, though knowing that Gwen would just tell her she was naive.)

'What did you have today?' said Laura.

'I presented with another boring duodenal ulcer but there was some suggestion from Guess Who that it might be a hiatus hernia. Heartburn anyway.'

'Worry?' said Laura.

'Probably,' said Mrs Donaldson, 'though the most recent research suggests that it can be bacterial.'

'That's right,' said Laura. 'I'm supposed to know that. About the money.'

'It's four weeks,' said Andy.

'Is it?' said Mrs Donaldson. 'I'm not sure,' and pretended to count. 'Yes, it's four weeks.'

'We've got one week,' said Andy and put an envelope on the table. 'We can't manage any more right now and the thing is we wondered if we could come to some agreement about the rest. Do something . . .' and he examined the inside of his teacup, 'in lieu.'

'You do so much for us,' said Laura. 'We wondered if we could do something for you for a change.'

'In lieu,' said Andy again.

Mrs Donaldson's thoughts were running to

18

housework, gardening and even painting and decorating, none of which she needed help with and certainly not to the tune of three weeks' arrears of rent.

'We talked it over in bed last night,' said Laura 'and it occurred to me that having seen you down at the hospital demonstrating we wondered if you would like it if . . .'

'We put on a demonstration for you,' said Andy. 'In lieu.'

Mrs Donaldson did not immediately understand. 'A demonstration? What of?'

Andy took out his diary.

* * *

'This used to be our room,' said Mrs Donaldson, 'when Mr Donaldson was alive.'

'We like it,' said Laura.

It was a few nights later and Mrs Donaldson had just drawn the curtains and with as much care (though for a different reason) as her mother would once have drawn the curtains in the blackout.

With regard to what was on offer Mrs Donaldson was still having difficulty bridging the gap between her first misapprehensions on the lines of bob-a-job and the something more . . . grown-up that was now in active preparation. She was far from looking forward to the prospect but was finding it hard to put off these well-meaning young people without seeming ungrateful.

'Have you ever seen anyone making love?' said Laura.

'To tell you the truth,' said Mrs Donaldson pretending to cast her mind back, 'I don't think I

19

have.'

'Oh good,' said Laura. 'We were bothered it might not be much of a novelty.'

'Oh no,' said Mrs Donaldson, 'it would. It would.' Though given the choice she still wasn't sure she might have preferred marigolds. 'No, I've never done anything like this before.'

'We haven't either,' said Laura. 'We've done it with other people around obviously, the way you do, at parties and so on, but never by prearrangement. Not . . . not . . .'

'Formally?' suggested Mrs Donaldson.

'Formally, that's it.'

'Oh it won't be formal,' said Andy coming in only in his shirt and underpants and with a bottle of water. 'It'll be very relaxed. Though I wouldn't want you running away with the idea we do anything particularly adventurous. It's good wholesome stuff, nothing . . . esoteric. We're not into that, are we, Lol? Not yet anyway.'

'Well the way I look at it,' said Laura, firmly, 'is that there is plenty of time for that in due course. Don't you agree?'

'Oh yes,' said Mrs Donaldson. 'All in good time.'

'Now, candles, candles,' said Andy and went out.

'Where would you like to sit?' Laura said.

'I don't mind,' said Mrs Donaldson, who was all the time thinking that there must come a point when she would pluck up courage and call a halt. 'I can sit here if you like.'

She perched on a chair at the foot of the bed.

'Fine, if you're happy with that,' Laura said, who suddenly had no top on or bra either so that seeing her Mrs Donaldson had to rummage in her handbag for a tissue.

20

'Except,' said Laura, 'the drawback with sitting there is that you're going to get an awful lot of Andy's bum and not much else. I think you'd be better off here.' And she patted the chintz-covered stool that stood in front of the dressing-table mirror on which, when she and her late husband inhabited this room, Mrs Donaldson used to perch every night to apply her cold cream.

'If you sit there,' said Laura, 'you'll see him and you'll see me like, you know, interacting.'

She disappeared into the bathroom leaving Mrs Donaldson sitting by the bed. At which point she had (and almost heard) that slow deep pumping of the heart she had not felt since she was a girl. 'Life,' she thought.

Andy now came in with three candles which he lit and disposed around the room, one of them Mrs Donaldson noted in a bowl they had been given as a wedding present, but she didn't say anything. Andy switched off the light.

'That's better.'

He took off his shirt though not his pants and lay on the bed, his hands clasped behind his head.

'This is awfully kind of you,' said Mrs Donaldson, wondering at the same time if they were going to take the coverlet off first.

'Don't worry,' said Andy. 'We'd be doing it anyway. It's not just for your benefit.'

He looked down his flat narrow belly to his exiguous underpants.

'Nothing much doing at the moment, I'm afraid. It's not a problem but I'm finding that's often the case these days. I have to wait until the dog sees the rabbit.'

At which point Laura came in bra-less as she

21

had been before but now with no pants on either. Naked in fact. Mrs Donaldson blew her nose as Laura lay down on the bed on the side nearest Mrs Donaldson.

'This is nice,' said Andy, lifting up his knees and arching his bum as he slipped off his underpants. 'There. See what I mean?'

Mrs Donaldson smiled in kindly acknowledgement of this new component of the scene.

Laura's left hand now rested lightly on Andy's right thigh.

'We generally fool around a bit to start with,' said Andy.

'Oh yes,' said Mrs Donaldson knowledgeably. 'Foreplay.'

Mrs Donaldson's first instinct was to look away so that rather than frankly considering this naked young man kissing his equally naked girlfriend with his hand buried between her legs she found herself looking at the floor and wondering if it was time she had the carpet cleaned.

'Bring back memories?' said Laura, Andy's face now where his hand had been.

'Ye-es,' said Mrs Donaldson, though the truth was it was a memory of a vase in the British Museum. In any case Laura wasn't listening, her body lifting itself clear of the insistent head.

Other things Andy was doing had not even been in the British Museum, and Mrs Donaldson found herself leaning forward and slightly to the side in order to take in what the young man was up to and where.

Though his face was largely buried between Laura's legs Andy's one unoccluded eye detected Mrs Donaldson's focus of attention and obligingly

shifted his head so that it rested against Laura's thigh, thus providing Mrs Donaldson with an uninterrupted view.

This unexpected démarche with its different angle on the proceedings provoked a series of harsh rhythmic cries from Laura coupled with violent squirming so that Andy, his application uninterrupted, gives Mrs Donaldson a thumbs up before raising himself on his arms and embarking on sexual intercourse proper with the unsignalled irruption provoking even wilder cries from Laura.

Standard sexual intercourse was a procedure with which even Mrs Donaldson was relatively familiar though pursued here with more vigour and variation than she had ever experienced herself.

Still in that the basic procedure was the same this at least was familiar ground, though Mrs Donaldson never remembered Cyril even in their earliest days going at it with comparable gusto and indeed verve, and whereas Andy gave vent to occasional whoops of encouragement and expressions of pleasure, with Mr Donaldson love-making (if it could be so called) had always been a stern, tight-lipped affair.

And yet it is what people do, she thought. Except this isn't what people did, she was sure of that. They didn't preside as she was doing sitting on her stool at the side of the bed where, observing the contending figures, Mrs Donaldson felt not unlike a tennis umpire overseeing a particularly close-fought match.

If the whole thing was a revelation there were lesser eye-openers. At one point with Laura on her back and Andy on top of her and both of them giving harsh cries almost in rhythm Laura's mobile went.

23

The cries stilled but, the rhythm unbroken, Laura stretched out her arm and took the phone. 'Bad moment. Sorry'—and the cries resumed.

Mrs Donaldson was surprised, though, how soon even the provocation of ecstasy began to pall. She marvelled at the undulation of the boy's body and back, as dolphin-like he plunged smoothly in and out on waves of passion. And at how supple they both were. Laura's legs now over his shoulders, a transition achieved without pause or disengagement.

Still, as she sat there, the witness to this spectacle, it occurred to her that she might be their mother (though whether his or hers she wasn't sure) somehow called in to testify to the full selfhood of her offspring . . . a mother who was kindly and forgiving (though what was there to forgive?) but knowing, too, that watching these young people so inventively entwined in one another was hardly within mothering's customary remit.

And then there was the money. It had all come about so easily she wondered if she was the first and if other creditors had been paid in the same tumultuous currency.

On her hands and knees across the bed Laura found her face only a foot or so from Mrs Donaldson's. They smiled.

'Men,' said Laura conspiratorially as Andy pumped and panted behind her. Mrs Donaldson smiled understandingly.

Whether Andy had caught this exchange and it was this that annoyed him Mrs Donaldson wasn't sure but he suddenly got much rougher, pulling Laura's head back by the hair and humping her

24

round to face the bedhead, the top of which he grasped so that it banged rhythmically against the wall; at the same time he began to shout and the girl, too, calling out with harsh expectant ascendant cries.

The Donaldsons' sex had been largely mute (and certainly posing no danger to property), a grunt from Cyril signifying that he at any rate had reached a satisfactory conclusion. On the few nights (and it was always nights) when Mrs Donaldson had had occasion to cry out Mr Donaldson had had to stop, claiming it put him off; the truth being that his wife embarrassed him.

These days they would probably have been advised to 'talk it through' but the constraints that can operate between couples would have made such openness unthinkable.

There was no embarrassment about these two, though, their shouts and cries loud and persistent and always seemingly poised just on the brink and needing some final push to take them over the edge.

This Mrs Donaldson unwittingly provided when, fearing for the safety of the table lamp (another wedding present), she placed a steadying hand on the bedhead thus giving Andy the degree of leverage he needed to bring the proceedings to a noisy finale. Laura took longer than Andy to quieten down, moaning still as he extricated himself to lie down beside her, both of them ending up side by side panting and exhausted.

Their congress concluded, the Donaldsons retired to their separate sides of the bed and went to sleep. There was never any discussion or comment even. It was over until next time.

Not so these young people who if an orgasm is a little death proceeded to conduct a post-mortem in an assessment of their respective quotients of gratification and pleasure.

Andy put his arm round Laura.

'What would be nice would be a cup of tea.'

Glad in this small degree to participate Mrs Donaldson went downstairs and since it was for her at any rate a bit of an occasion she put a cloth on the tray, used cups not mugs and opened some new biscuits. This was to some extent wasted effort as by the time she got back up to the bedroom they were doing it again but with no preliminaries this time and not much finesse, the boy heaving determinedly away, the girl lying back with her eyes closed.

Meanwhile Mrs Donaldson sipped her tea and ate a chocolate digestive biscuit and by the time they reached a second tempestuous conclusion she had had three and their tea was cold.

'I hope I didn't spoil your fun,' said Mrs Donaldson as Andy pulled on his jeans.

'No way,' he said and put his hand on her bum. 'If anything you added to it.'

Reflecting on the episode, which in the succeeding days she did a good deal, Mrs Donaldson decided that watching the young people make love was the nearest she had ever come to a deed.

True she hadn't been the one to suggest it and had only acquiesced and she wasn't sure that acquiescence was a deed. Marriage was meant to be a deed, for instance, and she had acquiesced in that though in retrospect it had turned out no more a deed than taking shelter from the rain.

Deeds came easier to some people than others,

she thought, almost effortlessly to some. She would have to try harder.

Seldom having had much of a secret before and never one of such intimacy, Mrs Donaldson was surprised at how strong the impulse was to share it, or at least to share the secret that she had one to share. She longed to tell Delia about the goings-on with her lodgers while at the same time knowing there could be no question of it and no hint ever. She was sensible enough to realise it was not an incident the couple themselves were likely to broadcast, the presence of such a middle-aged and respectable third party hardly a turn-on or an episode to boast about. Still, having a secret put her in a good mood, sheathing her against the petty annoyances at the hospital, the flirting of Ballantyne, the bullying of her daughter. Hectic though the evening had been for Mrs Donaldson in retrospect it constituted some sort of refuge, a haven utterly set apart, a place of her own.

'What are you looking so happy about?' said Delia in the canteen. 'Have the lodgers paid the rent?'

'They have as a matter of fact,' said Mrs Donaldson. 'We're bang up to date.'

'Is that what's bought the frock?'

'This?' said Mrs Donaldson. 'No. I've had this for ages. Just thought I'd give it an outing.'

'And a hairdo as well. Not to mention the lipstick. Jane, I think you've turned a corner.'

'No, no,' said Mrs Donaldson. 'You don't understand. It's work. I'm in drag.'

Parfitt, a sandy-haired spindly young man, was sitting at the table on the rostrum. Mrs Donaldson knocked.

'Come,' said Parfitt, who had heard this trope on the telly.

'Nice if you got up,' said Ballantyne from the back. 'Gentlemen do. And doctors are gentlemen. Or used to be.'

Parfitt gave Mrs Donaldson a chair and she sat down heavily with her legs apart and arms folded. She blew her nose on a large spotted handkerchief and said her name was Dewhirst.

'And your first name?' said Parfitt, pen poised.

'Geoffrey.'

'Geoffrey?'

'Yes,' said Dewhirst, 'with a G.'

Parfitt looked wild-eyed at the class hoping someone would help. No one did.

'We're waiting,' said Ballantyne. 'The patient doesn't have all day.'

Parfitt consulted his form.

'Have you always been called Geoffrey?'

'Yes,' said Dewhirst. 'Why?'

'It's an unusual name for a woman.'

'I'm not a woman.'

'Oh,' said Parfitt, sensing firmer ground. 'You're very convincing.'

'Thank you.'

'I would never have guessed.' Parfitt's manner was now kindly and professional.

'Is it a problem?'

'Not for me.'

'It's just that . . .' Parfitt pressed his hands together, 'I have to ask these things, get them straight.'

Somebody hooted, silenced by a glare from Ballantyne.

'Could I ask you something?'

28

'You're the doctor.'

'You've changed your appearance, gone to all this trouble, so why haven't you changed your name?'

'Why should I?' said Dewhirst. 'I'm not a woman. I'm a man.'

'So you've never had surgery?'

'Oh yes.'

'What did they do?'

'Cut me open. I had appendicitis.'

'I meant for your problem.'

'It's not a problem.'

'Oh,' Parfitt considered. 'So that's not what you've come about?'

'No. I've come about my knee.'

'Your knee!' Parfitt beamed. He knew about knees. Never had a knee been more welcome.

'Which knee is it? Shall we take a look.'

'Don't let's bother,' said Ballantyne. 'The knee is hardly the point.'

In the circumstances he was quite kind.

'We had to go all round the houses but we got there in the end.'

'I'd have known,' said Parfitt plaintively, 'only she doesn't look like a man.'

'Well,' said Ballantyne, 'we don't know what he is, do we? We only have his/her word for it.'

Parfitt still couldn't get it right.

'You mean I should have examined her?'

'No,' said Ballantyne patiently. 'You should have examined the knee.'

He came to the front and sat down. 'What you have to remember is that these days gender is in flux. The patient may be a transvestite, a transsexual or a transient on a park bench. It is

29

no matter. How they are dressed, how they look is of no clinical concern. The patient,' he smiled at Mrs Donaldson, 'may smell. His or her body may stink. That is not your concern either. If you want bodies that don't stink go in for surgery where they wash the patient first.'

He sat on the desk between Parfitt and the putative Dewhirst who was wondering if this performance was at least partly for her.

'Remember. You are a physician. You are not a policeman nor are you a minister of religion. You must take people as they come. Remember, too, that though you will generally know more about the condition than the patient, it is the patient who has the condition and this if nothing else bestows on him or her a kind of wisdom. You have the knowledge but that does not entitle you to be superior. Knowledge makes you the servant not the master.'

Ballantyne sat on the edge of the desk swinging his legs, now slightly sheepish. Tucked in at the end of the day and coming from a dispassionate and even sardonic instructor, to the class this sermon was unexpected and even inspirational. Just to be called a physician seemed a step up. It made the students think more of themselves than Ballantyne generally allowed them to do and some of them at least were reminded that this was not just a job but a calling.

Parfitt, though, was not one of them.

'Should I look at the knee?'

Ballantyne sighed. 'I think you should leave Dewhirst's knee well alone lest he/she take you over it and give you a good smack. Thank you, Mrs Donaldson. Another Oscar-winning performance.'

30

'You get all the juicy ones,' said Delia. 'I could have done him only what do I get . . . endogenous depression and no wonder.'

With her thoughts now never far from the session in the bedroom Mrs Donaldson wondered whether she owed her boldness (even if it had only been boldness in acquiescence) to the exercises in not being herself that she went through in the classroom. Without them she might have been less receptive to what was after all quite an outrageous proposal. Even so she had come close to dismissing the idea because 'she wasn't that kind of person'. But what kind of person was she? She was now no longer sure.

In retrospect she could see that the classes at the medical school, constrained though they generally were, had constituted some kind of preparation, a softening-up for what was to come and an unlooked-for initiation into candour even though the candour was put on and was not candour at all. She was playing a part both at home and at work, she was quite candid about that. She was learning to pretend whereas previously (when her husband was alive) the closest she got to pretence was politeness. Until now pretence with her had never been, as they said nowadays, proactive.

Having displayed themselves so unreservedly in the bedroom it wasn't surprising that the young couple and Andy in particular were more relaxed around the house. He was often without his shirt and occasionally his jeans and though Laura was more modest neither of them felt in the least inhibited.

Mrs Donaldson liked this as it made it seem more like home (though not one she had ever had)

31

until came the day when Gwen called unexpectedly to find Andy making himself some toast in the kitchen, and having that minute left Laura in bed, just in his underpants.

'I didn't know where to put myself,' she said to her mother, 'whereas he seemed to think it was perfectly normal. Took his bread and jam, said "Cheers" and went upstairs. Does she do the same? Parade about half-naked? Just some skinny little pants. I thought they'd gone out, pants like that. Our Justin doesn't wear them any more. Justin's gone back to boxers.' Justin being about as unbecoming as his mother, this wasn't a thought Mrs Donaldson wanted to dwell on.

'They live here,' she said apologetically.

'Correction,' said her daughter, 'they lodge here. I blame that hospital. Since you've started going there you've got really . . . lax.'

'Lax?' said her mother.

'I don't know what Daddy would think. You used to be so shy.'

'At least they don't play music,' said Mrs Donaldson. 'If they played music there might be something to complain about.'

'It seems to me,' said Gwen, 'you'd be quite in order making it a rule that whatever they do in the bedroom they keep their clothes on in the house.'

'A dress code, do you mean? They live here.'

'So do you.'

'They're company,' said her mother.

'How can they be company? They're eighteen.' They were actually twenty, but Mrs Donaldson didn't think there was any point in saying so.

Other than this loosening of the proprieties where the lodgers were concerned nothing

32

much changed. And of course the loosening was one-sided. Laura might slip downstairs in the minimum of clothing but not Mrs Donaldson. She understood instinctively that for her appearances must be rigidly maintained. She must be her age.

Since working at the medical school she had ceased to be intimidated by the young or, her lodgers apart, even to be interested in them much. Some were appealing, she could see that, but fishing for a diagnosis or floundering over her body they were too soft-shelled to make much of an impression.

In less vulnerable moments (i.e. when Ballantyne wasn't around) they were friendly enough, treating her she decided rather like their granny as 'a bit of a sport' (her word) or 'cool' (theirs) but never without a degree of condescension. Like the artist's model that daughter Gwen had identified her with, she was both there and not there, a frame on which to hang symptoms.

Dr Ballantyne put Mr Maloney in the picture.

'This is Mrs Dickinson. She has come to see her GP not for the first time about some recurrent eczema. Previous visits have not succeeded in uncovering any particular cause; all the usual remedies have been prescribed but the eczema always returns. Her GP has now begun to wonder if there is an underlying psychological cause, the eczema a symptom of a deeper malaise. Which is for you to uncover.'

Maloney nodded sagely.

'Good hunting.'

Dr Ballantyne laid a caring hand on Mrs Dickinson's supposedly itching and weeping arm before giving them both a wide smile and loping off

33

to another cubicle.

'I hate these mental jobs,' said Maloney and put one foot on the table. 'You never know where you are with them. Give me an old-fashioned tumour any day.'

'I'm sorry?' said Mrs Dickinson.

'Oh come on, love. This psychosomatic stuff. So you've got eczema. Wrong soap. Wrong washing powder. Diet, I suppose, maybe . . . there's generally a physical cause. But these days just for form's sake we have to go down the psychological route.'

Maloney's sights were set on surgery; all the rest was a waste of time. If eczema could be cut out on the operating table he'd have been interested.

'So. What's the story. How did she get it?'

'How did I get it?' the proto-patient primly corrected him.

Maloney sighed. This was one of the tiresome individuals who insisted on playing the game.

'It's not a spin-off from the menopause?'

'I don't believe I've had the menopause,' said Mrs Dickinson.

'Oh. So you're still doing the rounds. Maybe that's it?'

'I'm not still "doing the rounds" as you put it. I'm happily married.'

'Good for you. Hurray. Do you smoke?'

'No. And cigarettes wouldn't cause it anyway.'

'I know that, dear, I just thought we could nip out and have one behind the bins.'

'I'm in pain,' said Mrs Dickinson. 'I'm itching. My back is red raw.'

'Yeah yeah,' said Maloney.

'Tell you what. Why don't you give me the

34

upshot of the case, the conclusion you've got written down in your brief and then we can cut the whole business short. After all, even if it is all in the mind it's not going to make much difference. Nobody goes into dermatology, we all know that.'

'I've got a better idea,' said the supposed Mrs Dickinson. 'Perhaps we should get back to the case notes. And then you could ask me when this eczema first occurred.'

'She made me go through the whole rigmarole, stupid bitch,' said Maloney in the pub afterwards. 'Why should she care? I thought she was the one who was supposed to be cool.'

<p style="text-align:center">* * *</p>

Rent day was coming up again and Mrs Donaldson had been readying herself for the encounter. She had already decided that if a repeat performance was suggested she would feign reluctance on financial grounds before eventually giving in on the same terms as before. However on the Friday in question nothing was said until bedtime when Mrs Donaldson happened to be in the kitchen where Andy was making Laura a hot drink.

'Oh before I forget,' he said and brought out some £20 notes. 'I think this covers it.'

Not sure how many notes there were and not wanting to count them there and then she just smiled and put them in her bag.

'We're improving,' Andy said.

Mrs Donaldson left it a few minutes before she went upstairs and as she sat on her bed she thought she could hear them laughing.

Now she gets ready for bed, putting on her

dressing gown and not for the first time takes one of the flimsy bedroom chairs from beside the bed and puts it by the dressing table. Perched on the chair and with a blanket round her shoulders and an eiderdown round her legs she presses her ear to the wall.

Somewhere on the other side of the city Ballantyne is keeping his own vigil, running and re-running the tape he had taken months ago on his camcorder. Whenever Mrs Donaldson appears he freezes the frame, wishing he had the technology or the know-how to close in. Sometimes she looks directly at the camera and he feels she is looking at him and this is a small satisfaction. But mostly he just looks at her.

Mrs Donaldson's adventure had given her something of a boost. Though her own attractions had not been at issue in the scene of which she had been a witness, in some undefinable way seeing it (and to that extent participating) meant that she partook of the charms of the love-making couple. She imagined herself younger, she looked brighter, and ludicrous though she knew it to be, she felt she was still in the game.

But not for long.

Mrs Donaldson was not vain. She had never thought she was all that much to look at while at the same time recognising that she was probably more attractive now than she had been when she was younger. She was not petite and quite sturdy in fact but she had good skin, nice crisp hair that she kept neat and well-curled, and it was not surprising (and she was not surprised) if she appealed to men of her own age . . . women too maybe but she had no means of knowing that nor had any inclination

36

to find out.

Still, she was fifty-five, an age when should she take her clothes off full light was to be avoided, hotel bathrooms always dangerous places.

That the young people had not minded having her in their bedroom even from economic necessity meant a lot to her though had she had to participate, a wild speculation she these days entertained more and more, she would have been grateful for the candles. Fifty-five or not it had reassured her that she wasn't wholly repellent to look at.

The daily proximity of youth made this illusion difficult to maintain. She had been experiencing palpitations and periodic dizziness and someone in the first year had been put up to listen to her chest. This involved a slight loosening of her clothing—no more than a button or two of her blouse—a procedure to which normally and unless specifically required to behave otherwise she remained indifferent. But he was a handsome boy who undid her buttons with practised ease and she watched him as he listened to her heart. He was looking, too, and she caught his slight but unmistakeable revulsion as he touched the age-puckered skin of her breast which, since he was a bright boy, he was able instantly to convert into a frown of concern.

It wasn't quite quick enough to deceive Mrs Donaldson, though, who spotted it not as the patient but as herself and whereas she might ordinarily have taken some mild and wholly unacknowledged pleasure in his touch, now, looking at the unpuckered and slightly furred flesh of the young man's ear a few inches from her face, she felt soiled and withered and wholly without

value.

'Good,' said Ballantyne. 'But what did Mr Adams do wrong?' The boy looked suddenly crestfallen and Mrs Donaldson felt herself blushing. Ballantyne must have spotted his distaste too and now her carnal shortcomings were to become a means of instruction.

'Come along. How did he mishandle the patient?'

Various suggestions came from the class, all of them rejected.

Ballantyne sighed.

'Expert as I'm sure you are at undoing ladies' buttons, Mr Adams, you should allow the patient to do that for herself. Unless the patient is incapable . . . and Mrs Donaldson is certainly not that. You don't just go for it.'

The young man nodded ruefully.

'Otherwise excellent and even in such a routine procedure as this the patient has been left with her dignity intact. Thank you, Mrs Donaldson.'

'Conceited fart,' said Delia in the canteen. 'But face it, we're all of us curling at the edges. They never like my varicose veins.'

'I thought I'd got used to it,' said Mrs Donaldson. 'Does one ever?'

Once upon a time, i.e. before she had her secret, she would have let a setback like this depress her. Now it made her what Ballantyne would have called feisty and rekindled her animosity towards the young.

*　　　　*　　　　*

Prentice took his seat at the table on the dais. She

knocked at the door.

'Come in,' said Prentice.

Having come in she waited and Prentice got up.

'My name is Backhouse. I'm here to see my husband. He had a little fall this morning and they brought him in as a precaution.'

Prentice stood back from the table, looking at his clipboard.

'I know already Mr Backhouse is dead,' said Ballantyne. 'Or thereabouts. Why, anybody?'

A hand went up. 'When she came in he didn't look at her.'

'Quite so,' said Ballantyne.

'But does that mean . . .' this was another student, 'that he should have looked at her? Isn't not looking at her a way of preparing her for the fact that there is going to be bad news?'

'That depends,' said Ballantyne, 'on whether Mrs Backhouse picked it up. Let's see.'

'The nurse told me he wasn't here.' Mrs Backhouse looked at the young man. 'Where is he?'

'I'll just go and get a nurse,' said Prentice.

'No nurses available,' said Ballantyne. 'Nurses' outing. They've all gone to *The Sound of Music*.'

'Would you sit down,' said Prentice.

'I thought you'd never ask,' said Ballantyne.

'Mrs Blackhouse—' said Prentice.

'Backhouse,' said Mrs Donaldson. 'Not Blackhouse.'

'Mrs Backhouse. When your husband had his fall—'

'Look at her,' said Ballantyne. 'You know what's happened. Don't hide in your papers.'

'When your husband had his fall . . . Do you know anything about the brain?'

39

'Mrs Backhouse doesn't know about the brain,' said Ballantyne. 'She wants to know about her husband.'

'Actually I do know a bit about the brain,' said Mrs Backhouse. 'I was in the St John Ambulance Brigade.'

'I stand corrected,' said Ballantyne.

'Has he had a stroke?'

'Not exactly,' said Prentice, 'though there was some bleeding.'

'I know. I saw the blood. That's why I rang the ambulance.'

'We took him into intensive care but he went into a coma . . .'

'He's dead.'

Prentice looked at Ballantyne.

'You see, this is where a nurse would help.'

'Nurses still not back,' said Ballantyne. 'Gone for a fish and chip supper. Tea and bread and butter. You're on your own.'

'Could I get you a cup of tea?'

'Never mind tea. You haven't told her her hubby's gone.'

'He is dead I'm afraid. Would you like a cup of tea?'

Ballantyne groaned. 'There is no tea. There's been a power cut. The canteen is closed. Don't run away from her. Tea, a nurse, your clipboard . . . why are you hiding from this woman. She's your responsibility.'

'Is there anybody you'd like to ring?' said Prentice. 'You could use my mobile.'

'She's got one of her own,' said Ballantyne.

'Have you been married long?' said Prentice.

'A quibble,' said Ballantyne, 'but since he's dead

40

it's, "Had you been married long?" '

There was a giggle from the class.

Prentice took Mrs Backhouse's hand and someone guffawed. 'I don't know why you're laughing,' said Ballantyne. 'And why are you oafs nudging each other?' A grinning student at the back shook his head and did his best to look serious.

'Go on Prentice.'

'I think I'd just sit here holding her hand. Let her do the talking, you know,' said Prentice, 'only . . .'

'What?'

'What if it's a man?' said Prentice, 'and you can't hold his hand?'

'Arm round the shoulder? Christ, you're the tactile generation. Only no hugs, for God's sake. Just feel the situation. You're human beings, the majority of you anyway. There's no drill to sympathy.'

So Prentice sat for a while holding Mrs Backhouse's hand.

'He was a bastard,' said Mrs Backhouse.

'Come again,' said the young man.

'My husband. Mr Backhouse. A swine.'

There was a small whoop from the class.

'You're upset,' said Prentice.

'No, I'm not,' said Mrs Backhouse. 'I'm bereaved but I'm not upset.'

'It'll take time to sink in.'

'He's dead,' said Mrs Backhouse. 'It's sunk in. Twenty-five years of marriage is over. He's dead.'

Consolation no longer a requirement Prentice let go her hand.

'Can't help you, Prentice,' said Ballantyne. 'You're on your own.'

'Do you have any children?' said Prentice.

41

'A daughter. She'll want to know, I expect.'

'Will she be upset?'

'Oh yes. No more handouts. No more little lunches with her daddy. Oh yes, she'll be heartbroken.'

'Well,' said Prentice, 'I'm sure you will cope.'

He got up to bring this now rather distasteful episode to a close. He shook her hand in what was meant to be a consoling way though consolation had turned out to be redundant.

'If you stay here someone will be along with the necessary forms.'

As he was going Prentice turned back.

'I wonder . . . it's just a formality but what was Mr Backhouse doing when he fell?'

Mrs Backhouse looked at him.

'He wasn't doing anything.'

'Did he slip?'

'I don't know. I was upstairs. I heard a bump, came down and there he was on the floor.'

'The ambulance men say that they think he must have fallen off a stool.'

'He'd been trying to get something off the top shelf . . . it's where he kept one of his bottles.'

'Well,' said Prentice suddenly in command of the situation, 'there'll have to be a post-mortem. The coroner will have to go into all that.'

'Coroner?' said Mrs Backhouse. 'You mean an inquest? What for? I thought 90 per cent of all accidents occurred in the home.'

'So they do.'

She sat down again. 'I was upstairs. It wasn't my fault.' Prentice said nothing. 'Could I have that cup of tea?'

The performance concluded, there was unusually

some mild applause and with a few hollow-handed claps even Ballantyne joined in.

'Very good, Prentice, and very intriguing, Mrs Donaldson. I'm not sure how much it taught us about breaking bad news still less offering comfort to the bereaved but at least it reminded us that death and grief don't always go together: sympathy needs to be on offer but it's not necessarily welcome and can sometimes be thought presumptuous. The bereaved know the deceased whereas the doctor doesn't, and not knowing him or her is the doctor even entitled to offer his or her condolences? And of course it's just a formality but the genuinely upset may believe that formality is out of place and anything but heartfelt grief is hypocrisy. People are peculiar. I think'—and he looked at his watch—'that that is the real lesson.'

The class disperses, some of them smiling at Mrs Donaldson as they go.

'The children like you,' said Ballantyne. 'They think you're a bit of a card.'

'I like you too,' he wants to say but doesn't.

'You so regularly come up with the unexpected it's almost what one has come to expect. Here am I trying to teach them how to counterfeit compassion and you're teaching them something else.'

'What?'

'Honesty sounds too pretentious. Candour perhaps. Nothing to do with caring anyway.'

And he went off, ruefully nodding his head.

The truth was Mrs Donaldson hadn't given much thought to the scene they'd played. She wasn't in the mood to play the grief-stricken widow or to draw however crudely on the experience of her own bereavement. Her daughter's mourning had been

43

extravagant and her own, she felt, a bit perfunctory and even brisk so that in some sense the unfeeling response of Mrs Backhouse had a basis in fact. But she had never hated her husband, just got bored by him; a bottle on the top shelf might have added interest.

Then too, Delia had said Mrs Donaldson looked tired which, in view of her nightly sessions at the bedroom wall, was hardly surprising. So having a bit of fun with Prentice's fumbling attempts at caring was a way of proving Delia wrong. It was unexpected, she could see that and imagined this must be why some of the students had laughed. What did surprise her was how adroitly Ballantyne managed to extract some sort of lesson from what on her part had just been silliness and she saw again how, unprepossessing though he was, Ballantyne might still be a good teacher and she wished she could tell him so though without any of the complications ('Perhaps we could do lunch?') that would inevitably follow.

<center>* * *</center>

Rent day had come and gone with Andy paying so promptly and in such haste it seemed designed to avoid even the thought of a possible repetition. Disappointed though she was Mrs Donaldson found the money welcome and was also happy to be in a more settled frame of mind. True she still took up her station nightly but at the same time assuming that whatever transpired was now unlikely to include her.

The following week Andy had exams and tonight he was sitting downstairs revising while Laura was

ironing. Mrs Donaldson was taking advantage of their blameless occupations to read up on the next day's assignment before the stake-out that she would have to mount once they came upstairs. Frustrating though the circumstances might be it was still nice to have a routine.

She woke with a start finding herself slipping off her chair. It was well past midnight and she was cold. It was only when she'd got into bed that she realised that what must have wakened her was some sort of commotion going on. Now there was shouting on the stairs and suddenly her door burst open and the girl ran into the room trying at first to lock the door behind her. But she could hear the boy pounding up the stairs and terrified she ran to the other side of Mrs Donaldson. She was in one of his shirts which she pulled round herself crouching down as if to hide.

Mrs Donaldson was appalled. 'It's all right,' said Mrs Donaldson, getting out of bed to help her. 'What have you done?'

'Nothing,' the girl sobbed. 'Worn his shirt,' at which point Andy burst through the door just in his jeans saying 'Come out of there, you little cow.'

'This is my room,' said Mrs Donaldson weakly. 'Can't we talk this over?'

'No we fucking can't. And stay where you are. I want you to see this. Come here you—other way round. Do it.'

He got on the bed in the process kicking Mrs Donaldson on her bad knee as the girl crouched whimpering on the bed on her hands and knees.

'There's no need for this,' said Mrs Donaldson.

'There fucking is, isn't there,' said Andy and slapped the girl hard across her bum. She screamed

45

loudly.

'And shut the noise.'

The girl screamed louder and the boy reached forward to put his hand over her mouth.

Mrs Donaldson felt that she ought to get help, her first inclination to run out into the street and try next door or ring the police. Fetch someone, stop someone, anyone, to say come quick there's a girl being raped.

She got to the bedroom door.

'Where do you think you're going? Watch.'

The girl began to wail and Mrs Donaldson hid her face in her hands, and when she dared to look again the boy was having her on the bed. In the middle of it all the telephone rang and Mrs Donaldson thought she was saved except without stopping Andy leaned over and ripped the phone out of its socket, the vandalism causing Laura's screams to redouble and for Mrs Donaldson to wonder if rape was only the beginning of it.

It was blessedly short, ending with more shouting from him and loud cries of pain from her.

Then he lay down on his back on the bed, the girl whimpering beside him.

Wondering what the correct thing to say was after witnessing an assault, Mrs Donaldson said nothing. She was trembling.

'Well,' said Andy, clasping his hands behind his head, 'I think that puts us well into credit.'

'You hurt me,' said Laura.

'You hurt me. And I liked that shirt. I didn't catch you with my foot did I?'

'No,' lied Mrs Donaldson who was longing for a cup of tea and would have offered to make some

except that she was frightened that while she was downstairs they might make it up and begin again like they did the last time.

'I think you might have told me,' said Mrs Donaldson.

'Told you what?'

'That you were just pretending.'

'I wasn't pretending,' said Andy. 'Were you pretending?'

'No. I was frightened,' said Laura. 'You hurt me.'

'I'd had a sniff of something but nothing much. She deserved it. She'd fucked up my best shirt.'

'I can wash it,' said Mrs Donaldson.

'Oh, that's nice, isn't it,' said Andy. 'Isn't that nice?' And he put his arm round Laura and nuzzled her neck.

Mrs Donaldson didn't move.

The next day a neighbour came round saying they'd heard shouting in the night and was she all right?

'We nearly knocked on the door but it was one in the morning.'

'It was the students,' said Mrs Donaldson. 'Something and nothing. At least they don't play their music loud. They have these things in their ears now.'

'But you're all right?'

'Yes of course.'

'You must miss Mr Donaldson.'

Mrs Donaldson smiled bravely.

Gwen got wind of it, too, having run into a (different) neighbour in Waitrose, making Mrs Donaldson wonder if they had woken the whole street.

'Mrs Truman said she rang and got no reply.'

47

'The phone was off.'

'What were they doing in the middle of the night?'

'What do people do in the middle of the night?'

'Sex?'

'I imagine that came into it. I banged on the door and they soon quietened down. They're young.'

'That's what you always say. He's not violent is he, the boy?'

'Don't be silly. Anyway,' Mrs Donaldson cut her short, 'they're going soon.'

It was true. They had told her that morning. Andy had got the promise of a place at the architecture school in Edinburgh and Laura was taking a year out in Malawi.

'I hope you won't be getting any more.'

'Any more what?'

'Lodgers.'

'I don't know,' said Mrs Donaldson. 'I haven't decided.

'I shall miss them,' she said to Delia, though she could hardly specify why.

'They kept me on my toes.'

'Get some more,' said Delia. 'You never know.'

They were waiting for a session to start, sisters whose mother was in a coma.

'Never know what?'

'They might be nice.'

'I'm thinking about it. It will be good having the place to myself for a change.'

Good, too (though she did not say this), getting a proper night's sleep and having unfettered access to the bathroom. Not good was the absence of expectation and that she was back in her box again.

'Here we go,' said Delia as Partridge came in.

48

'Commence grieving.'

Partridge had called them in to ask their permission to turn off their mother's life-support machine. She had been run over and was now in a coma.

'I'd castrate them,' said Delia, whose name was Jackie.

'Who?'

'Hit-and-run drivers.'

'That wouldn't help,' said Mrs Donaldson's Cora.

'It would help me.'

'She was always stepping off the pavement.'

'Nobody is disputing that, Cora, only he didn't stop. I'd castrate him.'

'Castration isn't the issue,' said Partridge flatly. 'It's whether we switch Mother off or not.'

'Who are you calling Mother?' said Jackie. 'She's not your mother. She's Mrs Henderson to you. How do you know she's not going to come round? You're only about fourteen and you're not even wearing a tie. If you're going to condemn someone to death you might at least dress the part.'

Partridge looked unhappy.

'Besides,' said Jackie, 'look at these people you read about who've been unconscious for years then they suddenly come round?'

'Sometimes you have to take these decisions,' said Partridge.

'Why can't we just leave things as they are?' said Jackie. 'Wait and see?'

'There's nothing there,' said Partridge. 'She's brain-dead.'

'But she's alive,' said Jackie. 'And while there's life . . .'

'I'd let her go,' said Cora.

'*You* would,' said Jackie.

The sisters sat in silence.

'You see,' said Partridge to the back of the class, 'this is where a nurse would help.'

'You all of you keep asking for nurses,' said Ballantyne. 'Why?'

'A woman's touch?' said Culley.

'What if the nurse is a man?'

'It's still a shoulder to cry on.'

'Have you been on a ward recently?' said Ballantyne. 'Nobody will say this to you, but the truth is that at compassion, consolation and general humanity most nurses nowadays are crap. They can do the clinical stuff because that's what they've been taught, but when it comes to holding someone's hand, comforting the dying or a grieving relative, all the stuff that life should have taught them, nurses are useless.'

'But they're taught caring, aren't they?' said Partridge.

'Oh yes. They're taught it but it's life that should have taught them it. Experience. And just as you are too young to be doctors they are too young to be nurses. The best nurses are middle-aged, except they won't be nurses any more, they'll be administrators. So stop asking for a nurse when all you want is someone to do the feeling for you. If there's comforting to be done or consolation to be offered you're the doctor; do it yourself.'

'I work for an accountant,' said Cora. 'Am I right in thinking the basic problem is financial?'

'Well,' said Partridge, glad to have found someone sensible at last . . .

'I warn you,' said Ballantyne 'that if you say yes, Partridge, the other one is likely to put you on a

life-support machine yourself.'

'What has she got to live for?' said Partridge plaintively.

'Us,' said Jackie. 'Or me at any rate'.

Partridge sighed. Who switched the machine off wasn't his problem. He wanted to be a pathologist. The bodies he'd be dealing with would be dead already.

'Let's look on the bright side,' said Cora. 'If we switched her off it would reduce her carbon footprint.'

Jackie began to wail.

Partridge sighed.

'Well,' said Partridge 'we'll play it by ear.' He shook hands with the sisters. 'We'll give her another week or two.'

'No marks,' said Ballantyne. 'And nurses or no nurses you'll have to brush up on the humanity, Partridge. Currently that box remains resolutely unticked. Whereas you, ladies, are wasted at St Mark's. You should be on national television.'

* * *

Having lost her lodgers and even the sporadic rent they had provided, Mrs Donaldson found herself compelled to ask for extra sessions at the hospital. She tackled Ballantyne one lunchtime.

'My charm?' said Ballantyne. 'Or a new fridge-freezer? There are some slots but nothing juicy at all. Still it will be nice to see more of you. What have we got tomorrow? You don't want rectal bleeding do you, but that apart it's just gallstones, which is no challenge to Bickerton Road's answer to Meryl Streep.'

He handed over a folder.

'Unless of course you had a fit.'

'I had a fit not long ago,' said Mrs Donaldson.

'So you did . . . and memorably too. You could bring up your lunch, of course, but I think not. Let's keep it simple. Gallstones, it is.'

'Perhaps she's deaf,' said Mrs Donaldson.

'Or Latvian?' said Ballantyne.

'Diabetic,' said Mrs Donaldson. 'I know that inside out.'

'Good girl.'

Having thought it over Mrs Donaldson had decided, rent or no rent, against letting out the room. There would be no more nights with her ear pressed to the wall and none of the suffocating excitement that came every fourth Friday when the rent was due. It had been a holiday from respectability and not to be repeated, a one-off, the chance of her coming across any other lodgers as open-minded (and penurious) as Andy and Laura very slim. No. That chapter was closed. Regretful though she was, it had all been too much of a strain.

Still it left her with a curiosity, a prurience even, that, associating it with freedom, release and a new life, she was not now anxious to suppress. She had heard that there were all sorts to be seen on the internet. She didn't know about the internet but thought there must be courses one could go on: there were courses for everything these days though whether the instruction stretched to the kind of stuff she wanted to see she doubted. But, propriety preserved, that was what she thought she would do. Delia would know.

Having had a dullish day (thyroid deficiency, hiatus hernia and (non-extruded) piles), she was sitting in the kitchen having a quiet drink when the doorbell went.

Thinking it was probably Gwen, she whipped the glass into the cupboard before dutifully putting the chain on and opening the door.

'Mrs Donaldson?'

'Yes?'

It was a boy and girl.

'I'm sorry,' she said. 'I thought you were my daughter.'

'No. We've come about the room.'

He was wearing a thin overcoat, jeans and shirt and, surprisingly, narrow though it was, a tie. It was a look she thought she might have seen on TV, where she had certainly seen the hat, a silly little black, narrow-brimmed affair that was a size too small. It was the hat of a pop singer who was frequently arrested for drug offences, and though he had a sweet face the hat did nothing for him, making him look younger rather than older, which she supposed was its purpose, and not worldly at all.

The girl was more ordinary, big cardigan, long scarf, her only concession to fashion a shiny pink handbag.

'The room?' Mrs Donaldson said. 'What room? There is no room.'

Her decision to take no more lodgers had not been an easy one but confronted with this unbecoming pair she found herself relieved and even cheerful. No, no. They wouldn't have done at

all.

'You are on the list,' the boy said. 'I'm Ollie, by the way. This is Geraldine. I'm at the College of Art and Geraldine works in a café.'

'Organic,' said the girl, handing the lodgings list to the boy.

'Here you are,' said Ollie pointing out her name (fingernails quite clean).

'I told them to take me off,' said Mrs Donaldson.

'Well they haven't,' said Ollie. 'It's a shame since we've come all the way up from town. Did you have a bad experience?'

'I'm sorry?' said Mrs Donaldson.

'That made you take yourself off the list?'

'No, no. It's just that I . . . I thought I'd have a break, you know.'

'Couldn't you just give us a trial?' said the boy. The girl smiled wanly. 'Then if you like us you might change your mind. We could give you a reference. We know Andy,' said the boy, 'don't we?'

The girl nodded and hid in her scarf.

'Andy?' said Mrs Donaldson.

'Who was here before. We came round to see them once, only you were out.'

All this had been round the door but reassured as to their credentials Mrs Donaldson took the chain off.

'Do you see them?' said Mrs Donaldson. 'How are they?'

'Andy's in Edinburgh,' the boy said. 'Laura's in Africa somewhere.'

'Malawi,' said Mrs Donaldson. 'I had a postcard. Perhaps you'd better come in.'

The three of them sat round the kitchen table, Ollie still in his hat.

'We'd be very reliable with the rent,' said Ollie. 'Geraldine works in a café.'

'It isn't that,' said Mrs Donaldson.

'They weren't, though, were they?' said Ollie.

'Weren't what?' said Mrs Donaldson oblivious of the chasm into which she was about to fall.

'Reliable with the rent.'

'They weren't too bad,' said Mrs Donaldson. 'No. It's not that.'

'Is it us?' The boy smiled at her. He could have been fourteen.

'You?' said Mrs Donaldson. 'No. No. It's not you.'

'Anyway, they said you were very understanding.' The boy smiled. 'About the rent.'

Geraldine wound her hands in her scarf.

'We wouldn't have a problem with that, would we, matey?'

'No,' said the girl, her scarf in her mouth. 'No problem. No problem at all.'

'Excuse me,' said Mrs Donaldson. 'I've just got to go upstairs.'

She ran up to the bathroom, closed the door and was suddenly, surprisingly, sick.

She sat on the bed, their bed, and hid her face in the pillow.

It was something she had never imagined though now it had happened it seemed so obvious. If they knew, everybody knew, and she felt giddy with all the ramifications. The word would have gone round the medical school. And where better; she was a case herself. She felt beyond compassion and respect. A joke. 'Our landlady'.

She wiped her face and went downstairs.

They were sitting at the table, neither of them

55

speaking.

'I'll think it over,' Mrs Donaldson lied. 'I can't decide.'

The boy put his hand on her arm as they stood up.

'We'd be no trouble. Music and that.' He gave her a piece of paper. 'I've written down my mobile.'

She smiled reassuringly as if there was hope.

They stand on the doorstep and now for the first time the boy takes off his ridiculous hat and holds it against his chest in a gesture so old-fashioned she almost laughs, a pathetic waif whom the quest for accommodation has cast up on her doorstep.

'I like your hat,' she says.

He puts it on and behind his head a plane crawls across the sky and somewhere a woman is singing.

She comes back inside and sees on the table the slip of paper with his mobile number and next to it he has drawn a silly smiley face with a hat on it. Upstairs she lies on what had once been her bed, lies on it on the left which had always been her side.

* * *

And there at seemingly the end of what has turned out a cautionary tale, Mrs Donaldson could be left and readers wanting a moral ending should probably stop here and focus, as they say, on that suburban bed where the lady grieves for the sound and sensible woman she had once been and been thought to be, whereas the word that keeps coming into her head is bawd . . . a leering loose-breasted attendant on the pleasures of others.

She sees herself fallen into laughter and contempt and absented from all pardon and

56

understanding, her ordinary suburban home if not quite a brothel certainly a place of erotic trade, barter and exchange.

No, she should be left mourning everything she has so thoughtlessly thrown away.

Which would be all very well did she not still run and rerun her calloused recollections constantly in her head so that the (only two) scenes in which she had figured lose all colour, flavour and feeling; and then she runs them again. She knows the moments when had she not been so timid she could have intruded on the action herself even though this, for her momentous, intervention would have amounted to no more than laying her hand on the boy's lunging rump.

'He wouldn't have minded,' she tells herself, 'and probably wouldn't even have noticed . . . Still, one thing might have led to another.' And Laura similarly whose hand she might have taken and let it lead her into the action.

The preliminaries, too, she rehearses—the preamble in the kitchen, the preparations upstairs, the candles, the casual undressing: the whole sequence so familiar that in memory it becomes almost a ceremony. Her lodgers gone, it is what puts her to sleep every night and even on this fateful day, dismayed though she is and raw at the prospect of exposure, it's not a ceremony she omits.

But she thinks, too, of work, that old analgesic though one in this case that is no painkiller at all. She remembers incidents she had been puzzled by at the time—the unexplained laughter in class, the guffaws when Prentice had had to take her hand, the students smirking without apparent cause. Had she heard Maloney say 'I thought she was the

57

one who was supposed to be cool' she would have known. Now she did.

The next day she felt less chastened, mildly excited even, the actress in her quite relishing the bold face she was going to have to put on. Yesterday she had felt robbed of her necessary armour but this morning as she hung her coat in the locker she remembered one of her presentations on stigma and a woman whose face had been disfigured in an accident. 'I look at people,' she had had to say 'as if they were the injured ones.' So she put on a bold face.

Except that it hardly seemed to be necessary. Nothing appeared to have altered. If she was a laughing stock no one was letting on. Perhaps Andy and Laura had been more discreet than she was giving them credit for: they had told the boy in the hat and his glum girlfriend, it's true, but they were not part of the class or medical students even. Her disgrace might all have been her imagination.

Looking at the schedule Mrs Donaldson remembered that it was today she was to be working with Miss Beckinsale, whose undisputed province old age and its infirmities had always been. This dated from an early presentation of dementia that had so impressed Dr Ballantyne, it had seemed as rambling and diffuse as the real thing. Over the years Miss Beckinsale had contrived to annex contingent territories like aphasia and amnesia, strokes and other cerebral malfunctions. 'The mind', as she was fond of saying, 'and its encumbrances'.

Miss Beckinsale, though, was no longer young and some of her performances had got so wayward and self-indulgent as to be clinically unhelpful,

so that occasionally Ballantyne would steer some cerebral problem Mrs Donaldson's way: Alzheimer's of early onset, a couple of aneurysms and (very satisfyingly and a treat to perform) Tourette's. This last had been offered to Miss Beckinsale but she turned it down as it required her to blurt out obscenities she claimed never even to have come across. She hadn't heard of the disease either and when it was explained to her still wasn't convinced, putting it down to a lack of self-control.

The crumbling of her empire was not lost on Miss Beckinsale.

'Expect ructions,' said Delia. 'No trespassing.' Though to begin with at any rate the troupe's senior member seemed quite relaxed, even linking arms with Mrs Donaldson and whispering, 'Welcome to the mind.'

Ballantyne, too, had foreseen some genteel chuntering but when none was forthcoming, on this particular day he had ventured to team the two ladies in a scenario involving a daughter wanting to get her mildly demented mother into a home.

It was the afternoon.

'Are you the carer?' said Miss Beckinsale.

Mrs Donaldson sighed. 'No. Violet. It's Jane.' The students not having come in from their lunch hour, Mrs Donaldson wasn't having any of Miss Beckinsale's usual antics.

'We've not started yet, Violet.'

Miss Beckinsale shut her eyes tight.

'I don't start. I am! You're the carer.'

'I am not the carer,' said Mrs Donaldson. 'I am your daughter, Lois.'

'You? You're never my daughter. You're far too old for a start. And you wouldn't catch a daughter

59

of mine in a cardigan that colour.'

This was a typical Beckinsale tactic. Knowing no blame could attach, out of the thickets of her supposed dementia she fired spiteful little darts at her colleagues, one symptom of supposedly losing her mind her readiness to speak it.

Now the students were filtering in and Miss Beckinsale closed her eyes and let her mind drift at its moorings.

The student this afternoon was Metcalf, a stolid young man who thought geriatrics was a good area to get into, and now he joins the two women on the podium, shaking hands with the supposed daughter and ready to do the same with her pretend mother except that Miss Beckinsale, who was still getting into character, appeared not to see either Metcalf or his extended hand.

So he sits down at the table and makes a note.

'Now Miss Murgatroyd . . .'

'Mrs,' said Mrs Donaldson.

'I'm sorry,' said Metcalf. 'So there's a Mr Murgatroyd?'

'There was. He's dead.'

'She murdered him,' said her mother. 'Pushed him out of the window.'

'Prostate,' said the daughter.

'I don't even know her name,' said the old lady.

'What is your name incidentally?' said Metcalf.

'Lois.'

'It never is,' said her mother, 'her name is . . .' and Miss Beckinsale cast about for a name that would cause the maximum offence.

'. . . My daughter's name is Tracy.'

'Lois,' said Mrs Donaldson again.

Metcalf made another note.

'I'm going to ask you one or two questions to determine the degree of care Mother requires. Is Mother incontinent?'

'Only when she wants to be.'

'Does she soil herself?'

'When it suits her.'

'What is she saying?' the old lady said. 'Ask me not her.'

'I have to do everything for her,' said Lois.

'Interesting point,' Ballantyne's voice comes from the back of the class.

'When anyone says "I have to do everything for her" what they generally mean is that they have to do one thing for her.'

'She has men,' the old lady said, 'in droves.'

Ballantyne ignores this.

'It's also interesting,' he continues, 'that though a daughter can say "I have to do everything for her" about her aged mother, at the other end of life a mother would never say of her infant child "I have to do everything for her". Why do we take the helpless condition of infancy without complaint but not that of senility? Culley, any thoughts?'

Culley considered.

'The shit smells worse for a start.'

There was a shout of laughter in which Ballantyne does not join.

'It's a serious point. So it does. On you go.'

Metcalf persevered asking his textbook questions to do with memory, mobility and waking in the night but getting nowhere. It's plain that, mother and daughter, these are two awkward women. The mother wants to stay in her home; the daughter can't cope and wants her in a different sort of home. If they were in the least bit fond of one

another it could be heart-rending but they're not.

'Have you and Mother ever got on?' he asks.

'We get on,' says the mother. 'What makes you think we don't get on?'

'You've just called her a cow.'

'She's my daughter. I can call her what I like.'

Out of the blue Metcalf said, 'Who is the prime minister?'

'That feller,' she says. 'I know but I'm not telling you.'

'Can you take five from seven?'

'Why should I want to do that?'

Metcalf turns back to the daughter. 'You see Mrs Murgatroyd, it's pretty well accepted that elderly patients do better in familiar surroundings and this after all is Mother's home.'

'No, it isn't,' the mother chips in. 'It may look like my home and it may look like my street but they can do wonders with scenery nowadays. Quite frankly I think I'm in a home already only they're not telling me.'

Metcalf writes something down as Lois smiles understandingly.

'What it is,' says Miss Beckinsale, 'is that she wants a lodger.'

The class sits up.

With no mention of lodgers in the prep notes this, Mrs Donaldson knew, was another dart from Miss Beckinsale's personal quiver.

'She's lost her husband and now she wants a lodger.'

'I don't want a lodger,' said Lois. 'There's no room for lodgers.'

'That depends how you sleep,' said Miss Beckinsale. Somebody laughed. Mrs Donaldson

looked. Somebody else was grinning.

'They'll be doing that thing,' said her mother.

'What thing?' said Metcalf. 'That thing they do,' said Miss Beckinsale. 'Young people, old people' (a small whoop from somewhere); though it was a thing Miss Beckinsale normally never mentioned.

'You mean,' said Lois, 'the thing you had to do before you had me?'

'Don't be disgusting. I never did that. I never did that with anybody. I was a Sunday-school teacher. You did. You do.' And she banged on the table.

None of this was typical. Whatever her riffs and ramblings, Miss Beckinsale has always given sex a wide berth.

Liking banging the table she now does it some more.

Mrs Donaldson always has a bottle of water in her bag and under cover of the commotion and hidden by her bag she bends down and pours some of it under the table.

'Where did your husband fit in?' Metcalf is saying to the old lady. 'Did you get on?'

'Ask her.'

The water crept across the floor.

Mrs Donaldson smiled sweetly at Metcalf.

'I think Mother's had a little accident.'

'I never have,' said Miss Beckinsale, though whether as Mother or herself wasn't plain.

'She doesn't know she does it,' said Lois. 'She should be in care.'

'I'll get a nurse,' said Metcalf. 'To wipe up the wee. It's all right for a nurse to do that?'

'Yes,' said Ballantyne wearily. 'It's all right for a nurse to do that.'

As the class breaks up and while Miss Beckinsale

is ostentatiously 'coming down' Ballantyne takes Mrs Donaldson aside.

'Very good. Very good, though I'm not sure it entirely worked . . . Did Violet seem demented to you? I thought she was too much on the ball. Did she wet herself?'

'She didn't think so,' said Mrs Donaldson.

'Oh dear. Poor thing. Still, she is getting on and, though it's hardly a clinical judgment, these days she's often away with the fairies.'

'One thing I can't help noticing'—and he rested his hand lightly in the small of Mrs Donaldson's back, which she couldn't help noticing either—'I can't help noticing how, excellent as these scenarios always are, you perversely almost (because it's so unlike the real you) always choose to play the unsympathetic line—the uncaring daughter, the unforgiving widow. Your ladies are quite hard.'

'I'm not sure I can do emotion,' said Mrs Donaldson.

'In life,' which was bold for Ballantyne, 'or just in the lecture room? Are you still grieving?'

'Grieving,' said Mrs Donaldson. 'Who for?'

'Mr Donaldson.'

'Oh,' she said. 'Possibly.'

'Perhaps,' and his hand lingered on her back, 'perhaps I could take you out to supper sometime. It might take your mind off things.'

'What took him so long?' said Delia. 'I hope you said yes.'

Mrs Donaldson had said yes and with some relief since the invitation did at least prove that if her escapade with Laura and Andy was common knowledge it had not reached the ears of Dr Ballantyne.

This was the opposite of the truth. Having asked a student if she had ever seen anyone dead and received the reply 'only my hamster', Ballantyne had taken her and a couple of novices to mortality down to the mortuary for a view of some of the recently departed. Afterwards he had felt obliged to take the trio for a drink, which was partly restorative, but also because he had a review board coming up and he needed to plump up his entry in the staff/student interface box.

<p style="text-align:center">* * *</p>

It had been a stilted occasion ('Tell me, Rosemary, what is it that draws you to the bowel, which is normally a male preserve?') but the day had been saved by Nigel, yet another surgical aspirant who thought the prostate was a growth area ('Joke. Ha ha') and who, pursuant to his chosen speciality, breezily recounted legends of ancient sex. It was in the course of this rather tacky performance that Lockwood, who hadn't yet spoken and who in turn was thinking of his interface box and hoping Ballantyne wouldn't write him down as lacking in social skills, had felt he must make a contribution and so had told the doctor the rumours about Mrs Donaldson.

Both the other students knew apparently though Rosemary said she didn't believe it, and Nigel said Laura had told him so herself. Ballantyne said what business was it of theirs anyway and was surprised they hadn't got better things to talk about. There was a pause.

'Tell me,' Ballantyne said, 'where do you stand on the new polyclinics?'

<p style="text-align:center">65</p>

Betraying nothing to the students ('Mrs Donaldson is a professional through and through') and suppressing his longing for more information, Ballantyne far from being shocked found the news oddly encouraging. He had made his continuing interest in Mrs Donaldson clumsily and (as he knew himself) off-puttingly clear. That he had taken it no further could be put down to his own awkwardness where women were concerned but also to his timidity in the face of the self-possession and even superiority the widow radiated. Mrs Donaldson had frightened him a little. Now he was no longer frightened. When it came down to it she turned out to be no different from anybody else. He had been given a licence. They would have supper.

Reassured about Ballantyne, Mrs Donaldson had still been left in no doubt that Miss Beckinsale was in the know and by the sound of it everybody else. So she asked Delia outright, who it turns out had never been in any doubt.

'It's not fair,' Delia said. 'I'm ten years younger than you. Sex with the children, supper with the supervisor, where am I going wrong?'

'It wasn't sex,' said Mrs Donaldson.

'What was it then?'

So she told her, with the telling—and she realised this is what she had been missing— interrupted by shrieks of laughter from them both.

True, Mrs Donaldson edited the story, saying nothing about her nights by the wall, but telling the tale did not rob her adventure of its allure but rather the other way about, so much so that when she got home that night she went straightaway to the waste bin and delving among the dry teabags, cold rice and tomato skins she thankfully retrieved

the screwed-up scrap of paper Ollie had left her.

* * *

And so in due course the new lodgers moved in, with two weeks' rent paid in advance but no mention of any other conditions of tenancy or the flexibility of either party in the event of non-payment.

As lodgers they were even less obtrusive than Andy and Laura, seldom seen in the kitchen for instance, with Ollie seeming to subsist largely on takeaway pizzas.

Gwen was predictably unkeen.

'Does she ever speak? I've been round twice now and both times she's just scuttled off upstairs. He's chatty enough but what's with the hat? They look like buskers.'

'They're quiet enough,' her mother said. 'I scarcely know they're there.'

'A change from the last two. What's he studying?'

'Fashion, I think.'

'Fashion? Well, I suppose you ought to be thankful he's not gay.'

'There'd be nothing wrong with that,' said Mrs Donaldson primly. 'I've been someone gay at the hospital.'

Gwen groaned.

'What for?'

'Fun,' Mrs Donaldson wanted to say. 'A laugh. Or a penance for having landed the world with such a joyless creature as you.'

And yet, though she didn't care for her daughter, she knew that some of this resentment could be put down to the fact that Gwen was right.

What did she think she was doing at the hospital? What was she doing sheltering these two babes in the wood?

It was unseemly. Bold face though she put on, it wasn't her at all. But that was why she did it. It wasn't her.

No sooner were the lodgers installed than out came the eiderdown and Mrs Donaldson went back on sentry duty. It was an unrewarding tryst generally, with scarcely a sound coming from next door and so quiet that on one occasion Mrs Donaldson spent five minutes listening to them pumping away before she realised it was the sound of her own heart. Occasionally there was a muted wail which she took to be Geraldine but whether it was of grief or ecstasy it was hard to tell; it might have been sheer tedium.

For her part Mrs Donaldson began to wonder if the hint Ollie dropped at the start had not been a hint at all. Had she just misunderstood? Or was it a con, a way of getting a foot in the door and as soon as they were settled in not to be referred to? After all it wasn't something she could actually mention and it was not long before she began to feel she was making a fool of herself twice over.

Still there were less momentous contacts. Meeting her in the kitchen one evening Ollie said, 'Can I draw you sometime? Though I don't even know your name.'

'Jane,' said Mrs Donaldson. 'If you like . . . The drawing. How? When do you want to do it?'

'We can do it now, if you want . . . Jane.'

So she sat down at the kitchen table while he did a very creditable drawing of her plus some smaller sketches, sitting like a small boy with the tip of his

tongue between his teeth.

'There's a tradition of artists drawing their landladies or painting them. Did you know that?'

'No,' said Mrs Donaldson who was still not fond of the landlady category.

'Mrs Mounter,' said Ollie, all the time sketching. 'She was the landlady of a painter called Harold Gilman. Mind you she was an old lady.'

At which point Geraldine came into the kitchen and went straight out again.

'Enough already,' said Ollie. 'Only can I ask you again?'

<center>* * *</center>

'How do you want to do this?' said Ollie. He and Geraldine were sitting side by side at the foot of the bed, his hand holding hers. She looked unhappy.

'Shall I give you a shout when we're ready?'

As Mrs Donaldson turned to go Ollie said, 'Do you keep your clothes on?'

'Oh, I think so,' said Mrs Donaldson. 'I think it's probably easier, don't you?'

'That's what I thought.'

There had obviously been some discussion on the point.

'Gerry was bothered you might just dive in.'

'Me?' said Mrs Donaldson. 'Oh no. I'm just . . .' and she was going to say a fly on the wall but that was a bit close to the truth.

'I'm just an observer.'

The long-awaited call had come about an hour before. They had spent most of the evening in their room and hearing Geraldine's voice she took them to be arguing. But Ollie had come down to the

<center>69</center>

kitchen as she was making some scrambled eggs on toast. She had given him some and offered to do some more for Geraldine only eggs weren't her thing, apparently.

As she washed up and Ollie was drying he suddenly said, 'What about tonight? I know we've paid the rent but we could bank it. Andy and Laura used to do that, didn't they?' Mrs Donaldson agreed that they had, though without saying it was only the once. So while Ollie made Geraldine a cup of camomile tea she went back upstairs.

Ollie gave her a shout when the two of them were safely in bed and Mrs Donaldson went in and sat on the dressing-table stool.

Neither of them seemed in any hurry to get started, the boy sitting up against the bedhead with the sheet stretched across his flat belly just below his navel. Geraldine on the other hand had snuggled right down in the bed, peeping shyly at Mrs Donaldson over the top of the sheet.

'How are things in the café?' said Mrs Donaldson. 'Is it all organic?'

'Things in the café are fine,' said Ollie. 'It is all organic, isn't it, love?'

Geraldine nodded.

'Not bread,' said Geraldine.

'Not bread,' said the boy. 'It's wholemeal but it's not organic. What was Mr Donaldson like, your husband?'

'Ex-husband,' whispered the girl.

'Why?' said the boy. 'They weren't divorced.'

'He's dead,' whispered the girl as if this were a shameful fact.

'I know he's dead,' said Ollie, 'but that doesn't mean he's an ex-husband.' He smiled at Mrs

Donaldson and mouthed, 'Sorry.'

'Maybe,' he said, 'you don't like to talk about him.'

Mrs Donaldson didn't, particularly in these circumstances, but she just smiled as if it was of no consequence.

'How long were you married?'

'Twenty-five years.' It had actually been thirty.

'Nice.'

He eased down the sheet a little and the girl used the slack to cover her face completely.

'Gerry is a bit shy.'

'That's all right,' said Mrs Donaldson. 'So am I.'

'Hear that, Gerry? Mrs Donaldson's shy too.'

He stretched out his leg and rubbed Mrs Donaldson's knee with his foot. It was a nice foot, she thought, and more adult-seeming than his face. The toes were strong and sensible and the little toe not just an afterthought like hers. She was about to stroke his foot when Geraldine suddenly turned over and put her arm round the boy in the process dislodging the sheet altogether.

'Whoops,' said Ollie and quickly clapped his hand over his crotch and then laughed.

'I don't know why I bothered to do that,' he said, 'in the circumstances,' and took his hand away.

Mrs Donaldson smiled and tried not to take too much interest though registering he was more excited than he had let it appear.

'Your turn,' he said to the girl and unwound her from the sheet while she hid her face in his chest as he stroked her back saying, 'Easy, lovely. Easy.'

'Are you sure this is all right?' said Mrs Donaldson.

He nodded reassuringly and began fondling

71

Geraldine with more purpose, kissing her shoulders and running his hands down her back to her bum.

'You don't mind if we just get on with it?'

Mrs Donaldson shook her head, he gave her a thumbs-up sign and applied himself to the girl.

'This is what she likes,' Ollie said.

'No, I don't.'

'You did yesterday.'

'She doesn't want a running commentary.'

'Maybe she does,' said Ollie. 'Do you want a running commentary because I'm just about to slip my hand between my girlfriend's legs.'

She screamed, though Mrs Donaldson was relieved that it was with laughter.

Whereas Laura had flashed Mrs Donaldson the occasional smile and even winked at her over Andy's shoulder Geraldine, sternly and wholly absorbed with the job in hand, seemed in no mood for such incidental pleasantries. She never once even looked at the older woman and had Ollie not made up for it Mrs Donaldson might have felt a touch unwanted. But Ollie made every effort to row her into the proceedings, politely pushing Geraldine's knee down, for instance, so that the onlooker should have a better view of the action. And when he had Geraldine kneeling on all fours he leaned across and gave her hand a little squeeze saying to no one in particular, 'I really like this.'

The end when it rather lengthily came was less lighthearted with Ollie grim-faced and purposeful and Geraldine shaken by great shuddering sobs and the long despairing wail Mrs Donaldson had heard occasionally through the wall.

The action over, Geraldine went straight off to the bathroom as Ollie lay on the bed.

'I'm sorry,' he said. 'We should have had a pill first and she'd have been more relaxed. How was it for you?' And he grinned.

'It was nice,' said Mrs Donaldson, politely. 'I enjoyed it. Thank you very much.'

'I'm not sure it was value for money,' the young man said. 'I'd have liked a touch more abandon. Which there would be normally you know, one to one?'

'It's understandable,' said Mrs Donaldson.

He pulled the sheet back over him.

'How did it compare with Andy and Laura?'

'I think,' said Mrs Donaldson, 'that they'd done it before. Had somebody there, I mean.'

'Yeah? This is a first for us, as you could probably tell. Were we a bit awkward?'

'Oh no,' said Mrs Donaldson, 'that was what was refreshing about it. It was . . . genuine.'

'And what about Andy? How does it compare? You know, the thing itself?'

'Oh, I think they're much of a muchness,' she said untruthfully. And then she heard herself saying, 'I'd have to see them side by side.'

'Steady on.'

At which point Geraldine opportunely returned from the bathroom and Mrs Donaldson said goodnight, going back to her bedroom feeling rather pleased that she had managed to be a bit cheeky.

That apart, though, she didn't feel the session had been a success or quite the adventure she had been hoping for. Maybe the encounters were losing their novelty.

Waking in the small hours she thought she heard the girl crying.

73

A few (uneventful) weeks later Mrs Donaldson had a morning session. She was now working virtually full time, though having gone through the repertory of symptoms and situations, her homework at least was less burdensome than it had once been and she was seldom if ever at a loss.

A new term had begun and since this was the first year Mrs Donaldson scarcely knew any of them and nor was Ballantyne there to help. The initial stages of tuition had always interested him the least. True, the ignorance of the students gave him umpteen opportunities for sarcasm in which he was happy to indulge except that having begun by showing off a good deal he had got the idea (rightly) that this wasn't a side of him Mrs Donaldson much cared for. So with his self-restraint not always reliable he sometimes, as today, chose to absent himself from these early sessions altogether, which was easier when, as on this particular morning, the SPs were old hands. Terry was here with a strangulated hernia and another outing for his tangerine underpants, Delia with chest pains that might be a heart attack but which would turn out to be indigestion and Mrs Donaldson who had a bunch of indeterminate symptoms with which she regularly presented herself as suffering, she was certain, from cancer.

Mrs Donaldson wasn't feeling all that clever herself this morning and just before leaving the house she had been sick. She had taken a couple of tablets but now they were beginning to wear off and with Terry and Delia having been briskly disposed

of she found herself lying on a trolley in a hospital gown with two students in attendance and not feeling at all well, even, she discovered as she felt her tummy, in actual pain.

Without warning Mrs Donaldson suddenly began to shiver uncontrollably and so violently she might have been attached to a machine.

'That's a "rigor",' said the girl.

'How does she do it?' said the boy. 'It's amazing. Look, she's even sweating.'

'No worries,' said the girl. 'She's the crafty one apparently. Someone in the third year told me. Now dear,' and she bent over the trolley, 'what seems to be the trouble?'

'I'm ill,' said Mrs Donaldson, her teeth chattering. 'I was sick this morning. Get help. Get Dr Ballantyne.'

'All in good time. We'll just examine you.'

The boy fumbled his way round.

'Try and keep still if you can.'

He laid his hand on her abdomen and pressed at which she screamed out so suddenly he recoiled as if he'd been bitten.

'Bloody hell. No need to overdo it.'

Mrs Donaldson had left her folder on the chair and thinking to cut short the process the girl sneaks a look at what this quite spectacular bundle of symptoms is meant to represent.

Light dawned.

'No worries,' she said. 'It's all psychosomatic,' and suddenly she bawls in Mrs Donaldson's ear, 'You've not got cancer. This isn't cancer.'

'I'm so cold,' whispered the patient. 'Can I have a blanket? Get help.'

'We are help,' said the boy. 'This is what she does

apparently. She is brilliant.' Shivering and shaking and with her belly on fire Mrs Donaldson dimly remembered she had had to present something like this once before and she feebly beckons the girl closer.

'I think . . . I think it's acute appendicitis.'

'Really? Well that's good. At least it isn't cancer.'

'Help me.'

'Time's getting on,' said the boy. 'I'm supposed to be on a ward round in five minutes. Knock it off now, love. We've got the message. Oh God, she's pretending to be unconscious. Well, we're going to leave you to it.'

The students head for the door but as they are going the girl comes back and whispers in Mrs Donaldson's unconscious ear, 'It isn't cancer. Not cancer.'

Making his leisurely way back through the hospital Ballantyne ran into a distraught Delia who, thinking to collect her friend for coffee, had found her laid out on the trolley unconscious and unattended.

'You're a victim of your own reputation,' said Ballantyne visiting her on the ward the next day. 'But you were quite right. It was appendicitis. The rigor should have told them that, particularly when the pain was in the textbook spot. They'd no excuse.'

Ballantyne had had supper with Mrs Donaldson on several occasions but without ever touching her. Now, because she is or has been ill, he feels empowered to take her hand and stroke it therapeutically.

'I blame myself. I should have been there. Still, it will do them no harm to have come that close to

killing someone so early on in their careers. I made a lesson of it this morning and I said . . .'

Ballantyne having taken advantage of his position as doctor Mrs Donaldson now takes advantage of hers as patient and, seemingly weary, closes her eyes.

'You're tired,' says Ballantyne, reluctantly releasing her hand and falling back into the traditional doctor-speak he was always mocking in his students. 'Try and get some rest. We'll soon have you out of here.'

Scarcely had he gone when a more enlivening visitor arrived in the person of Ollie bearing an eccentric posy from the garden consisting of two sweet peas, a dandelion, a sprig of privet and a pigeon's feather, an assemblage which, having put it in her tooth glass, he proceeded to draw while sitting on the end of her bed. He took her hand, too, which made her glad he wasn't with the listless Geraldine, who, unsurprisingly, had a thing about hospitals.

Ollie wanted to see her scar and was disappointed to find it was still hidden by dressings or he might have drawn that too.

'Never mind,' he said. 'Plenty of time for that,' and promising to keep the house tidy, was off.

Gwen was her other visitor and though the full circumstances of the students' negligence had been kept from her she renewed her efforts to get her mother to find employment elsewhere or, better still, abandon employment altogether. This was in between floods of tears since, as she took pains to make clear, this visit was for her particularly poignant as she had not been in the hospital since her father died. She was explaining this to her

mother, but, as she told her indifferent husband later, 'Mother seemed very tired. Slept most of the time I was there. It reminds you she won't always be with us.'

Back at home for a brief convalescence, to begin with Mrs Donaldson resisted the temptation to resume her nightly routine. After that first unsatisfactory evening it seemed unlikely that there would be a repeat performance and no necessity for it either as Ollie had paid the rent on time and in full.

Perhaps her brush with mortality ought to have turned her thoughts to worthier objects, but it hadn't. What was putting her off was Geraldine. Her diffidence and the general drabness of her disposition displeased Mrs Donaldson if only because it tended to take the edge off her nocturnal vigils. Though still occasionally *en poste* she was now less conscientious about it, once knocking off in the middle of an encounter that gave no sign of coming to a conclusion and since she knew the conclusion was likely to be Geraldine's melancholy, long withdrawing wail she felt she was better off in bed. Also, she told herself, she'd had an operation.

She reflected that what had briefly been almost suffocatingly exciting was now routine, as routine in fact as it had been when Mr Donaldson was alive and she was still a participant. She didn't like to feel like this—it seemed a portent of age. Morality had nothing to do with it.

It meant though that any relief from her mural duties was welcome and when Geraldine had to go over to Halifax to stay with her sister Mrs Donaldson was glad to get back to an early bed and a nice read.

*　　　*　　　*

Earlier that evening she and Dr Ballantyne, or Duncan as she was now licensed to call him, had been out to supper. He talked about his life and his career and when it got to the coffee stage he asked her to marry him.

She had been expecting this and while she could not give him an immediate reply she had an answer ready which was that, flattered and grateful though she was, this proposal had come as such a surprise she would like to think it over.

Emboldened by her ambiguous response and also remembering what he had been told of her goings-on with the lodgers he went a step further and placing his hand on the inside of her thigh suggested that it might help her towards a decision if they were to go to bed together.

This proposal too, was not unexpected, her first line of defence her not long-removed appendix and the presumed need to treat her recently perforated abdomen with some consideration. This he lengthily pooh-poohed delivering a long lecture on the body's recuperative capacities and pointing out that in any event there were other intimacies short of penetration that would involve no pressure on the particular muscles in question.

This she had not foreseen but fell back on the quick thinking she had learned in the classes saying that she might have been persuaded had not today been a special day, citing it as the (entirely spurious) anniversary of her late husband's death. If only out of respect for Cyril could their encounter be postponed . . . Duncan?

79

Duncan put his hand over hers. 'If there was anything you could have said that might make me respect you more this is it. Of course we will wait. We must wait.'

It was a harmless lie but back at home and having an early bed she thought that were this a novel it might ultimately have found her out: should he ever mention it to Gwen her cover was blown.

She thought, too, about marriage. It would mean knuckling down. Marrying Mr Donaldson she'd had to knuckle down though there hadn't been much to knuckle down from. Marriage to Dr Ballantyne would mean knuckling down, too . . . though this time there was more to lose.

She was reading her book and about to turn her light off when there was a gentle knock at the door.

It was Ollie, just in his T-shirt.

'I was wondering if you wanted to come in.'

'But Geraldine's not here.'

'Yeah, I know. She's had to go over to Halifax. Her sister's poorly. She may be there for a week or two.'

He waited.

'What do you think?'

'Besides,' said Mrs Donaldson, 'you've paid the rent. You paid it on Friday.'

'Yeah. Missed a trick there. What do you think?'

She put her book down and took off her reading glasses.

'I'm not sure.'

'Yeah? Why not?'

'It's just that I'm nearly at the end of this chapter. But if you just give me a minute or two, I'll come in.'

'Are you sure?'

80

'Yes,' said Mrs Donaldson, putting her glasses back on. 'No problem.'

THE SHIELDING OF
MRS FORBES

Like many a handsome man, Graham Forbes had chosen to marry someone not nearly as good looking as himself and even slightly older.

'Chucked himself away if you ask me,' his mother said. Which of course, he didn't. 'Waste, waste, waste. I'm his mother. I'm good looking. Naturally one assumed he'd marry someone along the same lines. We've always been so close.'

'My chum,' she called him. 'My young man'.

'We told each other everything. Or I thought we did.'

Graham's father having nothing to say, said nothing.

'I feel such a fool putting the announcement in the paper. I mean, "Betty".

'What sort of a name is that? Margaret, yes. Joan, possibly. Though I must confess Caroline was the least I'd been hoping for. But Betty!'

As names one might think Betty and Graham nicely matched, both dull and unassertive and not committing their bearers to any particular stance on human affairs in the way that Tessa does, or Rory even. But this was partly the trouble. For, though she could never admit it, Graham's mother blamed herself for calling him Graham in the first place. In the years since he was born her sights had risen and Graham was not nearly the classy name she'd once thought. She wished now that she could get rid of it as she had got rid of the dark oak dining suite that belonged to the same period. But though car-boot sales exist to dispose of discarded aspirations there are no stalls dealing in our most unwanted commodities like names, relatives or one's own

appearance in the glass.

'I wouldn't care,' said Graham's mother, 'but her first name's only the half of it. Look at her second name: Green. Betty Green. I wouldn't put it past her to be Jewish. I've known Green be a Jewish name.'

'It's actually Greene,' said Graham's father. 'Like the novelist. There's a silent "e".'

Graham's father was understandably sensitive to this spelling, being something of a silent he himself. Indeed his wife was often taken for a widow. She had so much the air of a woman who was coping magnificently that a husband still extant took people by surprise.

'I believe he's a Catholic.'

'Who?' said Graham's mother.

'Greene. The novelist. It comes up in his books from time to time.'

'Oh,' said his wife. 'I wouldn't want my son marrying a Catholic.'

For Graham's mother there was little to choose between Jews and Catholics. The Jews had holidays that turned up out of the blue and the Catholics had children in much the same way.

'I suppose she could be a Catholic,' said Graham's father. 'I could see her as a nun.' The idea seemed to please him but it didn't please his wife.

'Just our luck she missed her vocation. I mean face facts, Edward. He's very good looking; she isn't. Marriage is supposed to be a partnership. Good-looking people marry good-looking people and the others take what's left.'

'There's always love,' said Mr Forbes lamely.

'Love,' snorted Mrs Forbes. 'Of course there's

love. She's in love with him, who wouldn't be? But what does he see in her?'

'She may have money.'

'A hole in her cardigan and the same tights three days running? I've seen no sign of it.'

'Her parents are dead.'

'That doesn't stop her going to the dry cleaners. If only she'd had some parents we'd have a better idea.'

'She does have parents,' Mr Forbes pointed out patiently. 'Everyone has parents. It's just that hers are both dead.'

'So she claims,' said Mrs Forbes. 'They probably took one look and abandoned her on a hillside somewhere, the way they do in stories. Orphans, I don't trust them. Didn't we see something like that at the Playhouse?'

'*Oedipus*,' said Mr Forbes. 'Only that was ancient Greece. This is Alwoodley.'

'Ancient Greece? They were wearing suits,' Mrs Forbes said. 'He was in a sports car.'

'That was the production,' said Mr Forbes.

'And he had a mobile phone.'

Mr Forbes gave up the struggle and switched to silent mode.

Mrs Forbes's suspicions notwithstanding there was no mystery about Betty's origins. Betty was a genuine orphan, her parents both having died when she was in her teens. So far as the marriage was concerned she was trying not to think about them too much: they might have liked Graham; they would certainly have liked his father; it was with his mother they would have drawn the line.

'I'm going to feel such a fool on the wedding day,' said his mother. 'And to think I've looked

87

forward to it ever since the day he was born. He's always been so fastidious. I've known him spend half an hour choosing a tie. And he has no end of shoes. It's such a waste. And God knows what the children will be like.'

'I suppose . . .' mused Mr Forbes.

'You suppose what?'

'I suppose they've . . . had it off.'

'I beg your pardon?'

'Done it. Got his leg over.'

There was a pained silence. It was an ancient battleground . . . what she called it, what he called it and whether he was allowed to call it anything at all.

'I suppose you mean "made love". Because I prefer not to think of it.'

'She's probably,' said Mr Forbes, warming to the fray, 'a bit of a goer.'

'A goer? Edward. When are you going to learn that there are certain phrases you cannot use?'

'I've heard Graham use it.'

'Graham is different. Graham is young, attractive and drives a sports car. He has a life with the top down and language to match. He can say "guy" and "bird" and "cool", all the things young people say. You can't. I heard you say "tits" the other night at the Maynards'. You're too old to say "tits".'

'What age is that? When is the cut-off point? How old does one have to be still to say tits?'

'It's not just a question of age. Some people can say it all their lives. Whereas you, you've never had enough dash.'

'Oh. Dash is it now?'

'Dash. Flair. Brio. All the qualities that come to Graham naturally.'

88

The irony was that though Graham's father was much less particular about whom his dashing son chose to marry, like his wife he would have been much happier if Graham had not married at all, though for different reasons. Graham married would leave his father in the entirely undiluted company of his mother, a prospect he dreaded and that she was now envisaging too.

'With Graham gone at least we will have the chance to get to know one another again. You could introduce me to this internet you're always buried in. After all, life is for living.'

Mr Forbes who had just made a new and unseemly friend in Samoa saw all his cautious little world about to be kicked over.

He shut the door carefully and settled in front of the screen. Better make the most of it. And here at least he could say tits.

When Mr Forbes wondered if Betty had money he was right. She did. And Graham knew because he worked in a bank.

'He does not work in a bank,' said Graham's mother. 'He is in banking.'

He had met Betty when she had come in for advice after her father died.

'These what you call shares,' said Betty, 'Dad seems to have quite a collection. There's even some from Japan.'

'This is the stock market, Miss Greene,' said Graham. 'It is not philately. Let me be the first to congratulate you. You are a rich woman. Bereavement apart, you are laughing.'

'I don't understand,' said Betty, who understood perfectly well but thought how nice his hands were.

'Would you like me to explain?' said Graham.

'If it's no trouble,' said Betty.

To be taken in by this degree of ingenuousness one has to be pretty ingenuous oneself.

'He's such a straightforward boy,' said his mother. 'I blame myself.'

One does not have to be in the forefront of the struggle for women's rights to find Betty's decision to marry Graham deplorable. She wasn't wholly infatuated, though she liked the way he looked; but, so too did he and that unfatuated her a bit. Still, she could be forgiven for thinking that her money entitled her to someone out of her own league. Besides she liked her maiden name no more than her future mother-in-law did. It was time for a change.

Handsome as he was, for Graham their association was not without its humiliations. He drove, as has been said, a sports car and if it was being serviced his garage lent him an old Ford Escort. Drawn up in his vehicle at the traffic lights Graham was painfully aware of the pitying looks of other drivers.

They were the same looks he got, he imagined, when he went out with the plainish Betty and it was to avoid such embarrassment (and because he was very fond of his car) that made much of what Graham's mother called 'their courting' both nocturnal and motorised.

They were parked in a beauty spot.

'Your mother blames me,' said Betty, undoing his belt.

'She'll get over it,' said Graham lifting himself up in the car seat so that she could ease down his pants. 'After we're married I think we should have a joint account.'

'What's that?' asked his wife-to-be and though this was supposed to be the first one she'd seen she meant the account.

'It's just an arrangement so's you won't have to come running to me for money every five minutes.'

'And the reverse,' thinks Betty. 'Kiss?'

'To begin with,' said Graham, 'then just sort of use your imagination.'

Betty having no parents to make the arrangements for her it fell to Mrs Forbes to oversee the preparations of the wedding, a burden which she shouldered reluctantly, only too conscious of its tragic irony. Still she felt a church ceremony was essential if only to demonstrate that the bride was neither pregnant nor Jewish. But that an occasion to which she claimed to have looked forward half her life should turn out to be a public humiliation seemed almost a punishment.

'I can just see the looks on their faces,' she complained to the dressing-table mirror. Weddings were critical occasions and had to be carried off. Though hardly popular she had a wide circle of like-minded friends, many of whom would be only too pleased to see her discomfited, and a tear ran down her cold-creamed face. Mr Forbes, sitting up in his pyjamas with his laptop felt a pang of sympathy, though it was soon dispelled.

'Have you talked to Graham?'

'Not yet.'

'Not yet? What sort of a father are you?'

'It has to be in church, I suppose?'

It was a question no one had thought to put to the bride though Betty and to some extent Graham would have been quite happy with the registry office. But mindful of his mother and also of the

presents Graham thought they should make the effort.

'At least it's not a white wedding,' said Mrs Forbes, heaving herself into bed. 'She's so dark people might think she was Asian.'

'If it has to be in church,' said Mr Forbes, 'I hope it will be in accordance with the Book of Common Prayer.'

'What else should it be in accordance with?' said Mrs Forbes. '*The Highway Code?*'

'It may have escaped your notice,' said her husband, 'but the services these days are different. For a start one has to shake hands with one's neighbour.'

'In my recollection,' said Mrs Forbes, 'one seldom had a neighbour. There were only ever about four people there.'

'Then they'll have to go at least twice because of the banns. I hope . . .' said Graham's father (and this time choosing his words carefully), 'I hope they know the facts of life.'

'Graham is twenty-three.'

'That won't deter Canon Mollison.'

The vicar was old. The chief love of his life was the steam engine, and his version of the facts of life which he had been dispensing over many years relied heavily on the piston, the furnace and the eccentric rod, helpful did one want to travel from London to Darlington but no preparation for the rigours of modern marriage.

*　　　*　　　*

Mr Forbes seldom saw his son on his own. They had never been out for a drink together, for instance,

92

or to a football match as fathers and sons are supposedly wont to do. Graham was so much his mother's child that the father tended to think of him if not quite as his mother's agent then certainly her roving reporter and so was always somewhat wary in his presence. Morning suits being in order Mrs Forbes sent the pair of them off to Moss Bros to get kitted out. It was an awkward occasion made more so by it being assumed that as father and son they would be happy to share a dressing room.

A shy man, Mr Forbes had seldom seen his son undressed since he was a boy and even more seldom had Mr Forbes allowed himself to be so seen. The suits in question were hung up waiting and Graham, emboldened by the presence of several full-length mirrors briskly stripped down to his underpants. Mr Forbes was more tentative and it was only when he was reluctantly in his shirt tails that he found his dress trousers had gone missing. So while they were located he sat miserably on a bench feeling both wizened and portly and tucking his veinous legs as far as he could well out of view. It was an unnecessary precaution as Graham scarcely noticed his father, altogether absorbed in his several reflections and the trousers which he felt were too loose to be properly becoming. It was at this point with Graham standing in front of the mirror arranging and re-arranging his genitals that Mr Forbes remembered his wife's instructions.

'Your mother thinks that you and Betty should go and see the vicar.'

'What for?' Graham put his hand down his trousers to try dressing on the left.

Mr Forbes looked down at his inadequate legs. He needed to ask if his son and his fiancée

93

had made love but since his son was his wife's representative he phrased it accordingly.

'Has the engagement been consummated?'

'Frequently.'

'Your mother says you mustn't tell the vicar that.'

'I imagine he'll have the good manners not to ask.' Mr Forbes looked away as Graham took off his trousers, unashamedly loosening his crotch in the process. Actually the truth was they hadn't done it yet, though they'd done just about everything else but he was unlikely to say that to the vicar or to his mother either.

Mr Forbes's trousers now arrived and with them a greater degree of parental boldness.

'If you are getting married in church, Graham, the vicar likes you to pretend you believe in God. Everyone knows this is a formality. It's like the air hostess going through the safety drill. God's in His heaven and your life jacket's under the seat.'

'I don't see what that's got to do with whether we've done it or not.'

'When you are as old as Canon Mollison,' Mr Forbes said patiently, 'one of the few perks of the job is talking to young people about the sexual act. What in any other context would probably get him arrested, in the vestry passes for spiritual advice.'

'It must be a very depressing job,' said Graham.

Still, he looked wonderful and reluctantly taking leave of the mirror he briefly inspected his father. He would do.

So in due course Graham and Betty went to church and the banns were read and they had the session with the vicar. When they came out Betty burst out laughing, which she had been wanting

to do inside (Graham had just been bored). Now she made Graham see the funny side of it so that Graham, who had never come across a woman who made jokes, realised, almost for the first time, that he might actually like her.

<center>* * *</center>

On the night before his wedding Graham was in bed with a youth called, he thought, Gary. Gary was well built. His smooth flesh was cool, hard and perfectly proportioned, and contemplating the silent back Graham decided it was like the flesh of heroes as described in classical mythology.

'And they didn't have much in the way of small talk either,' mused Graham. 'No,' he said.

'Mmm?' murmured the youth, half-asleep.

'Just thinking aloud,' said Graham. Was his name not Gary but Trevor? Graham tried half-saying the name to himself. No response. The smooth back rose and fell. Of course many people (many boys he meant) didn't thank you for saying their name. In these circumstances, names tended to be left off along with everything else.

Gary stroke Trevor had a silver chain round his neck from which hung a thin, oblong medallion. It lay now somewhere between his chest and the pillow. It was likely, Graham reasoned, or at least possible that this slip of metal would carry its owner's name, so, stealthily stroking his way to a different district of the vast back he began to edge the medallion round into view. He was relying on the young man being asleep as such a manoeuvre was not easy to disguise, fiddling with someone's identity disc hardly to be incorporated into, or

<center>95</center>

interpreted as, any form of love play known to Graham, though curiosity about everything attached to his companion's person must surely count as a compliment.

Graham lightly lifted the chain free of the young man's neck, and gently pulling it round he eased it free of a low-lying curl. Even his ears were perfect, at any rate the one he could see, neat, simple, the lobe furred with a faint, fair down. Slowly the nameplate edged into view, faintly misted from the heat of its wearer's body. One side was plain: Graham turned it over.

'Shirley,' the young man said. 'I fuck her on Fridays.'

'Is that nice?' asked Graham.

'She thinks so.'

'Why Fridays?' asked Graham.

'Her hubby plays squash.'

There was a pause while Graham thought about Shirley and the young man.

'You like that,' said the boy.

'What?'

'Me and Shirley.'

'Why?' said Graham,

'It feels to me you do.'

'Actually,' said Graham, 'I was just looking at your back.'

'Yeah. I swim. Stroke my bum.'

Graham did so though somewhat abstractedly wishing he could remember the name of its owner. Still, it wouldn't do any harm, Graham decided, to make it plain that he too had irons in other fires.

'I'm getting married in the morning.'

'Ding dong the bells are going to chime,' said the putative Trevor.

'How do you know?' said Graham, who was not into musicals. 'It might have been in a registry office.'

'Allow me to wish you every happiness. Actually, though, not there. Just where my bum joins my legs. It's one of the lesser-known erogenous zones.'

At the word erogenous Graham decided he couldn't be called Trevor and began to lose interest a little.

'In fact,' the young man went on, 'I think I maybe discovered it. If my bum were an orchid it would probably bear my name.'

This was hardly the down-to-earth lorry driver ferrying a load of hard core from Rochdale to Penzance he had earlier claimed to be.

'You seem very articulate for a lorry driver.'

'I read, don't I. In lay-bys. When you see lorries parked in lay-bys that's what they're doing nine times out of ten. Reading. What's she like? Pretty?'

'No,' said Graham honestly.

'Big tits?'

'Not particularly.'

'Expecting?'

'No.'

'So what're you marrying her for?'

'There are other things,' said Graham primly.

'Oh sure. Don't stop. I like it. It's my favourite thing.'

Graham wearily complied but changed the subject.

'Great flat.'

'Yeah.'

'Quite classy.'

'I like it.'

'And the shower is great.' They had sampled the

97

bathroom earlier. 'Pricey?'

'I manage. So,' and he put his head on his arms, 'no more of this then?'

'Oh, I don't know,' said Graham. 'I shall just have to play it by ear.' See what I can get away with was what he meant. A good deal, he fancied, as the disparity between Betty's looks and his own gave him plenty of room to manoeuvre; it would be some time before she ran out of gratitude; that was only fair.

'I suppose in the circumstances this is your stag night?'

'You could call it that. What kind of lorry is it you drive?'

'A big one.'

'Not a juggernaut, I hope. I disapprove of those on environmental grounds.'

'Well,' said the bum without a name, 'we have to get the goods from Point A to Point B. This time tomorrow night I shall be in Penzance.'

'I shan't.'

'You don't have to stop at my bum. One thing is supposed to lead to another. That's what it's all about. I don't think your mind's on this, Toby. You're thinking of Miss Right.'

Graham wasn't. His thoughts were in the usual place and he was wondering why he should be the one to have to do the stroking.

'On balance,' said the supposed Trevor, 'I prefer it straight. You get through more energy. It's the post-coital rabbit I can't stand. Turn over and I'll do the same for you.'

As Trevor, whose name was actually Kevin but who had said it was Gary, stroked the back of Graham's legs he wondered whether Toby thought

this was for free. The question had not been discussed in the bushes where they had met but Kevin which was to say Gary got the feeling that Toby which was to say Graham thought he was doing him the favour and wondered how he might make this misconception plain. Still, as he lightly stroked the underside of his partner's buttocks in the feathery way that he himself preferred he felt a glow of self-satisfaction that he was doing to someone else what he most liked having done to him.

'I don't like that,' said Graham. 'It tickles.'

Abandoning Toby's ticklish bum the young man turned on his back, clasping his hands behind his head. His armpits were top scorers, too, thought Graham, though in what context he could not imagine. Butlin's possibly, or Channel Five.

'Do you like your name?' Graham said.

'Gary?' said Kevin. 'Yes. Yes I do like my name. In fact,' and he raised himself on one elbow and looked down his body, 'I like everything about me. My feet, my belly, my face . . . and, of course, that. I've never had any complaints anyway. And while we're on the subject I think it's about time you did something about that, Toby.'

'All right, Gary,' said Graham, now that the body beside him had a name, feeling his ardour rekindled, 'what would you like me to do, Gary?'

'Be my guest, Toby,' said Kevin. 'Oh, and in the circumstances, the wedding and so forth, this one's on the house.'

*　　　*　　　*

The wedding the following day went off without

a hitch, the vicar, having previously noted the disparity in looks between the bride and groom, pronouncing it a most Christian marriage.

The bride's side of the church was only thinly populated even with some of those syphoned off from the overcrowded pews on the groom's side. Betty's parents had been elderly and most of her surviving relatives were elderly too and reluctant to make the journey north. It was unsatisfactory but as Graham's mother reasoned had Betty's family turned out in force it might have confirmed her suspicions about her daughter-in-law's racial ancestry.

There were no bridesmaids, what few women friends Betty had not really bridesmaid material. This was another blessing as the risk with bridesmaids is that they are prone to point up the inadequacies of the bride.

'Not difficult in this case,' thought Mrs Forbes. Or Mrs Forbes senior as she now was.

Where the best man and the ushers were concerned Graham was spoiled for choice and a bevy of high-spirited young men gave the occasion an element of whoopee it might otherwise have lacked.

Still, some of their reactions were unexpectedly heartfelt and at the climax of the service the best man was seen to brush away a tear, a gesture not seen by Mrs Forbes, who was too busy weeping herself, the happiest couple of all and wholly untearful not Graham and his bride so much as the bride and Mr Forbes, whom she had chosen to give her away. They were radiant.

At the reception both Betty and her new mother-in-law were surprised by what good dancers

many of Graham's friends turned out to be even if Graham himself took the floor reluctantly, doing a dutiful round with his mother and then with Betty but thereafter leaving it to his friends, many of whom seemed quite happy to dance on their own.

The unlikely king of the floor, though, was Mr Forbes. He had always been a good dancer; indeed it was one of the reasons why Mrs Forbes had picked him out. These days he seldom got the opportunity to show off his talents but as he waltzed his wife elaborately around the floor it was plain that, despite having overfortified himself with champagne, he had lost none of his skill and together they made an impressive couple.

This was deceptive. The drink had emboldened Mr Forbes and made him uncustomarily combative and he used the freedom of the dance further to explore the permitted limits of his sexual vocabulary.

'Balls?' he quickstepped. 'Scrotum?'

Mrs Forbes stony-eyed gave no indication of having heard but maintained throughout a fixed and ghastly smile as her now foxtrotting partner remorselessly plied her with smut. 'Pussy? Fanny? Arse?'

He might have been murmuring endearments in her ear and it could have been a touching spectacle. Certainly as the number ended the guests broke into spontaneous applause which Mr Forbes acknowledged as holding his wife's hand she gracefully curtseyed. She had never been so unhappy in her whole life.

*　　　*　　　*

Having just bought a flat into which they were anxious to move straightaway the happy couple had forgone a lengthy honeymoon in favour of a weekend at a country-house hotel.

What Graham chose to call their 'fooling around' had been virtually unrestrained and surprisingly enjoyable and all with some sort of vehicular setting ... the front or back seat of the car, his or the more commodious model belonging to his father. That they had never, in Graham's words again, 'gone all the way' was partly because he was, if only in regard to the opposite sex, quite old-fashioned but also because he had never even in the alternative sphere been into penetrative sex and wanted to put it off as long as possible.

That apart it might be thought strange, his sexual inclinations being what they were, that Graham had never had any worries about the physical side of things. This, though, is to forget how much in love Graham was with himself. True, a mirror was always a help ... a real mirror, that is; Graham did have his own full-length mirror that travelled with him wherever he went. No one else could see it, of course, but without it he was nothing whereas with it all things were possible: he could have faced a firing squad if he could have watched himself doing it. And though this wasn't quite the spirit in which he approached his wedding night he was looking forward to seeing himself perform. However, when he surveyed their sumptuous quarters in the hotel he realised this was not going to be easy.

In many of the hotel rooms Graham had stayed, not always alone, an artfully located mirror afforded a reflection of the bed, the vision of himself naked on the sheets sufficient in itself

102

to excite him with or without a companion. Here it was plush; grand and lavishly furnished with genuine antiques, the side table piled high with copies of *Country Life*, *Tatler* and *The Field*; one lacquer box contained after-dinner mints, another a selection of the Prince of Wales's biscuits, plus, courtesy of the management, a basket of fruit and a huge bunch of peonies. What there was not was a mirror. There was a massive wardrobe, it's true (bird's-eye maple, French, nineteenth century), but there was no mirror.

Nor were there, as Graham swiftly ascertained while Betty was in the bathroom, any porn channels on the TV. On his travels for the bank Graham was used to staying in hotels a notch or two down from this palatial establishment where, though the accommodation might be less well accoutred, porn was always on offer. There, too, the rooms were smaller and the walls were thinner so that one could sometimes catch the occasional hint of what might be going on next door. Here the swagged drapes, the damasked wall covering, the refectory table, the royal biscuits all proclaimed the establishment's indifference to such unworthy considerations. Honeymoon suite though it might be and the lap of luxury that it certainly was, good taste prevailed and sex was not catered for.

The reflection problem (of which Betty was unaware) was unwittingly solved when hanging up some of her clothes she opened the wardrobe to reveal that the interior of the door was backed by a full-length mirror, so once she was in the bathroom Graham with a little experimentation worked out that fully opened the wardrobe door would give a decent account of what, all being well, would be

taking place on the bed.

So when Betty emerged from the bathroom it was to a ready and waiting Graham with the role he chose to play that of the stern and unsmiling husband now at last taking possession of his territory. 'This,' he said as he cast aside his towel, 'this is when the marriage begins in earnest.'

Which it did with Betty abject and submissive and to begin with at any rate their conjunction wholly satisfactory.

Except that as he gazed sideways in admiration at the rise and fall of his buttocks the vigour of the assault caused the wardrobe door to close slightly leaving him with an unappealing reflection of knees and ankles. He twice had to get up and correct this (with no explanation offered to Betty) but when it happened a third time he decided to forget the mirror and just get on with it. From his new wife's point of view this was preferable not simply because she now had her husband's undivided attention but because deprived of the stimulating spectacle of his own heaving buttocks Graham took appreciably longer in reaching a conclusion.

Lying post-coitally naked on the bed Graham considered his wife and himself. He had seen a good many bodies in his young life though few that came up to his own. Since the stakes between him and his partners had seldom been equal, sex generally involved a degree of condescension on Graham's part which in a nicer or less vain man might have been counted as compassion. But not with Graham.

This is where love generally comes in: whether the inequality between the partners is physical or social or indeed financial, evening up the score is

what love is about. Still, even in the most perfect of unions there's often detectable an element of bestowal. And that Betty was of the wrong gender made making love to her seem to Graham the greatest bestowal of all. He turned towards her again; it was actually quite enjoyable.

<p style="text-align:center">* * *</p>

For a marriage that might be thought to have little going for it things actually went very well. It helped that as a cook Betty was good and also inventive; her mother-in-law had been neither so when Graham arrived home from the bank and there was always a delicious meal to be had it was a novelty. Nor did Betty object to him spending the whole of the evening in front of the television; in fact there was very little Betty did object to so that her young husband found himself even more pampered than he had been before.

At work, too, he was prospering, marriage having reassured his superiors at the bank of his seriousness and his dedication and (though this had never been mentioned) his sexual inclinations.

Betty had come along to one or two of the bank-oriented social occasions, grim affairs which she seemed to enjoy and where, out of earshot of Graham, she had impressed his colleagues with the pertinence of her questions: if she was sceptical of the answers she took care not to show it. 'Your good lady seems to have her head screwed on,' said Graham's project manager. 'She's not just a pretty face.' Since she certainly wasn't that Graham took no notice anyway. He did, though, make it plain that he now did not actually need the job which

naturally made his superiors all the more eager to offer him a better one.

In other respects too, there was no cause for complaint. Once the novelty had worn off it might have been expected that marital sex could quite soon have lost its charm. Not a bit of it. The truth was Graham found a great deal more to do when making love to Betty than he ever had with the most enterprising of his male partners. Moreover there was a burglarious aspect to doing it with Betty which he had never come across before.

There were the clothes for instance. Had a young man in the past insisted on keeping on his trousers thus leaving Graham to negotiate zip, buttons, pants and whatever else, he would have found the corresponding preliminaries with Betty more familiar. But such slow divestment was an apprenticeship he had never had to serve, his partners gladly casting off whatever they had on the quicker to enjoy Graham's charms. So now, coming home from the bank (and sometimes without even taking off his coat) he gets one in with Betty before supper; he finds the fumbling attendant on her urgent and only partial déshabillé particularly exciting as it comes always with the sense that he is breaking in. It's a sense she contrives to give him but Graham is not sophisticated enough to know that. The obstacles were also natural ones bred out of unfamiliarity with the geography of the region and the function of its components. Women, he found himself thinking, had to be investigated. But mouth clamped to mouth while he fumbled around below he had the entirely pleasurable notion that he was cracking a safe. Though he never failed to effect an entry the combination still remained

a mystery, with married love for Graham still pleasingly felonious.

If any precautions in the way of condoms and suchlike have gone unmentioned that is a casualty of the storytelling. Though the slithering on of contraceptives has been elided in this narrative, in his premarital sexual sorties Graham had been scrupulous never to omit this preliminary even when giddier bedfellows mocked his circumspection. This, though, should have come as no surprise as however frantic the foreplay the neat fashion in which Graham put his shoes by the bed with his socks tucked inside should have signalled that this was not exactly a free spirit.

However, here again married love had its untransgressive attractions. Since Betty was on the pill or took precautions of her own which Graham did not choose to enquire into, the marital bed was untrammelled by tedious prophylaxis so that what Graham had been expecting to find an onerous and even distasteful duty unexpectedly partook of a freedom and absence of restraint that he found exhilarating. He took to his home sheets with unsheathed abandon; here at least he wasn't going to catch anything and the assurance lent his efforts both confidence and flair. Betty, whose sexual expectations had not been high, found herself the object of prolonged and vigorous and on the whole pleasurable assault. She was astonished at her husband's verve and gusto but if she was astonished there was no one more so than Graham.

Elsewhere Mr Forbes had not been allowed to forget his despicable behaviour at the wedding and he spent several months in more or less permanent exile to the garden shed. In his wife's brief absences

from the home he managed to get to his computer and send hurried (and always lying) bulletins to his grass-skirted friend in Samoa. But now he had a new friend.

<p style="text-align:center">* * *</p>

In the months immediately following their marriage Betty busied herself with furnishing and kitting out the newly bought flat. Firmly rejecting her mother-in-law's offers of help, with Mr Forbes she was more approachable. Though she was herself a dab hand at the computer Mr Forbes was useful in other respects, particularly in locating and shopping for her various requirements. Besides being good company he was also something of a handyman so more and more he could be found making the trip over to his daughter-in-law's where they both shook their heads over their respective partners.

Mr Forbes had retired early, his pension tied to the price of shares in his former company. The resultant fluctuations in his income were a constant source of anxiety to Mr Forbes and finding him often groaning over the stock market Betty eventually persuaded him to tell her why and to take her through his portfolio. Though he felt he was only indulging her curiosity Mr Forbes found Betty surprisingly knowledgeable ('I used to have to do this for my father') and within a few months (and with a lot of laughter) she had so restructured his retirement settlement as to virtually double his income, the only proviso being that he should mention it neither to Graham nor (which was much the same) his mother. Graham's notion of a wife was as an ingenuous dependency and knowing

<p style="text-align:center">108</p>

much more than he did she had the sense to keep it quiet. Not for the first time Mr Forbes wondered why a woman so decidedly accomplished had chosen to marry his son.

One of the functions of women, Mr Forbes had long since decided, was to impart an element of trouble into the otherwise tranquil lives of men. His wife, for instance, though almost alarmingly robust, claimed to be seldom altogether well, though it wasn't anything one could put one's finger on. True the trouble was often to do with that department Mr Forbes might have been expected to put his finger on but rarely did while at the same time being something intangible which, unless the man kept it in the forefront of his mind, allowed him to be accused of a lack of consideration and of being heartless. What was wrong, Mr Forbes felt, even with someone as stalwart as his wife was that the man was not perpetually aware that there was something wrong. That was what was wrong. Perhaps Mr Forbes's experience was unfortunate and if this was indeed a flaw of the gender it was one Betty wholly lacked, as she was cheerful, funny and, as Mr Forbes remarked to his wife, 'full of the joys of spring'.

'Who wouldn't be, married to Graham?'

Nor did Betty impose any of the linguistic dos and don'ts which so trammelled frank and open discussion with his wife. 'Balls' figured, 'arse' and the occasional 'Shit!' and greatly daring he even ventured on 'fanny' (at least in its derivative of fannying about). Betty was not in the least put out. Mr Forbes preferred being called Ted but Mrs Forbes thought Ted Forbes sounded like a character in *The Archers* and always called him

109

Edward. Betty, without being told, knew enough about her mother-in-law to call him Edward when she was around and Ted when she wasn't. It was all part of licensing him to be the bit of a devil he felt his wife had never allowed him to be.

Graham, of course, had been a bit of a devil in his time though if Betty has any inkling of his premarital inclinations she keeps her observations (it would be wrong to call them suspicions) strictly to herself though their life together was not without clues.

Thinking Betty was in the bath Graham was watching a late-night programme on Channel 4 called *Footballers with Their Shirts Off* when she unexpectedly came in on the trail of the hair dryer.

'I didn't know you were interested in football,' said Betty.

'I keep an eye on Newcastle,' said Graham just as (in an old clip) Gary Lineker swapped his shirt with some dish from the former Yugoslavia.

'I prefer him now,' said Betty.

'Who?'

'Gary Lineker,' said Betty. 'Grey hair suits him. Still, nice legs.'

'I wouldn't know,' said Graham primly.

'Funny programme,' said Betty. 'Is it recorded highlights?' and went back to drying her hair.

'Should we have a child?' The question is Betty's and they are in bed.

'Isn't that a bit of a shot in the dark?'

'I wonder about starting a business?'

'What sort of a business?'

'On the internet.' She'd already done this but hadn't said so to Graham.

Graham was silent.

'I have to do something with my life, Graham.'

'You have done something with your life. You've married me. I'm the one who has to do something with his life. Why don't you take up photography?'

Betty sighed.

'Could we go to bed again?'

'Betty. We are in bed.'

'You don't like me to say the word.

'Make love. Say "make love".'

<center>* * *</center>

To say that Betty had entertained no suspicions of Graham's premarital sexual experiences suggests that this is what they were, premarital. This was not entirely true. He still had the odd fling, now more of a treat than it once was partly because it was rarer but also because it was more risky and so seemed to him bolder.

On one of these occasional forays Graham found himself in bed with a well-proportioned young man who, while devoting himself wholeheartedly to the business in hand, still managed to give the impression of being a not unamused spectator.

'So Toby . . .' and the naked young man put his hands behind his head. 'How're you surviving the rigours of married life?'

The question was post-coital and mildly disturbed Graham, who had been smart enough to leave off his wedding ring.

'All right,' he said diffidently.

'All right? All right? I don't like the sound of that. Mind you,' and he looked down at the equally naked Graham, 'I think it's got bigger. Filled out a bit, know what I mean?'

<center>111</center>

It began to dawn on Graham that they had met before and the name suddenly came to him. 'Gary.'

'Aww you remembered.' Kevin gave his thigh a squeeze. 'Your stag night, right?'

'You're the long-distance lorry driver.'

'No, no. Your memory is at fault there, Toby. I'm the panel beater.'

'Your hands are very soft for a panel beater.'

'I apply a protective cream.'

It was all coming back to Graham.

'You've gone up in the world.'

'You think so?'

'This place, it's a gated development. Last time you were just in a flat.'

'Nothing but the best,' said Kevin, stroking his belly, 'only Toby—you set too much store by material possessions.'

Not a panel beater, thought Graham. An interior decorator, maybe.

'How's Shirley?'

'Who?'

'Shirley,' said Graham. 'Your girlfriend. You fuck her on Fridays.'

'No such person. I couldn't have anything to do with a girl called Shirley, Friday or any other day of the week. I'm not sure I'd even get it up.'

Graham noted that Gary had exchanged his chain and label for a pair of dog tags.

'These are new,' said Graham.

'Only to you. I like them. They add that whiff of combat. We could be in the Falklands. Or a tent in the Western Desert.'

He was leaning on his left elbow idly tracing a circle round Graham's navel.

This wasn't a scenario Graham had much

112

interest in pursuing. He and Betty had once done it in a tent overlooking Nidderdale, and area of outstanding beauty though it was it had not been a success and a vile tea in Pateley Bridge had not redeemed it.

'I hope you're being diligent and conscientious in the performance of your marital duties. Is she still getting it twice a night?'

Graham who was not dissatisfied with his record in this department smiled complacently.

'She know you play for the opposition?'

'Yes' would have been the prudent answer.

'No,' said Graham. 'No idea.'

'Would she mind, do you think?'

'Of course not,' said Graham, learning from experience. 'Not these days.'

'That's right, Toby. What's gender? Spread it around.'

'Time I was off,' said Graham.

He reached for his clothes neatly folded on the bedside chair.

'Don't fancy a supplementary?'

Graham looked at his watch.

'Can't I'm afraid.'

'She won't mind. Tell her you were kept late at the bank.'

'I didn't say I worked at a bank.'

It's true he hadn't, but casting his mind back he couldn't remember where he'd said he worked. 'You're in a bank. I'm a panel beater. That's how society works. Speaking of which I'm afraid I'm going to have to charge you for this one. Shall we say, £100.'

'A hundred? Fuck me.'

'I wish I could say I just had but that's where you

113

draw the line, Toby, remember?'

'You're lucky I've got it,' said Graham, handing over the notes. 'I don't carry much cash.'

'Why should you?' said Kevin. 'You work in a bank. Nice car.'

Coming away Graham felt uneasy. Had he said he worked at a bank? Had he said which bank? It was this element of risk that was supposed to give these encounters their edge but this time Graham didn't like it one bit.

Besides it was expensive. The gates slid open.

Back in the room Kevin was feeding the number of Toby's new car into his mobile.

* * *

For the moment things are looking good for the Forbes family. Graham's marriage is more satisfactory . . . and more satisfying . . . than he could have hoped and he is also making progress at the bank, playing squash with executive clients, sitting in on property deals which, it's true, he doesn't always quite understand but which his wife with a few seemingly naive and common-sense questions helps him to sort out without jeopardising her status as 'the little woman'.

Meanwhile Betty's internet business thrives. For the moment the question of a baby has been shelved though the actual shelves are still being taken care of by Ted, which is to say Mr Forbes senior.

If there is an absentee from this general felicity it is Graham's mother. Naturally she sees much less of Graham married than she did him single. Occasionally he has supper at home if Betty is

going out to a concert, say . . . she is a keen music lover . . . a passion she doesn't share with her husband ('I prefer light classical') but which she has communicated to Graham's father who sometimes escorts her, thus leaving mother and son to indulge in their old relationship. But however much she enjoys such occasions they also bring home to Mrs Forbes how empty her life has become.

Once upon a time Mrs Forbes had had hopes of the internet, thinking it would serve as a substitute or, as she put it, 'a hobby'. These hopes, though, have gradually petered out as she has proved persistently incapable of mastering the technology.

'It's really quite simple,' said her teacher, patiently, but since her teacher is her husband he makes sure that essential keys remain unpressed and connections unmade.

'It's a man's game,' he says kindly, which, bearing in mind the use to which he puts it himself, is quite true, the snake-hipped dusky beauty in Samoa (but who actually lives in Clitheroe) safely sequestered from Mrs Forbes's questing but untutored fingers.

Kindlier women than Mrs Forbes might have taken some consolation in an expectation of grandchildren but there seemed to be no sign of them and looking in the mirror and smoothing down her plaid skirt over still shapely hips Mrs Forbes doesn't feel quite old enough for that yet anyway. Instead on these long afternoons she dreams, sometimes rehearsing a scene in which she receives news of her husband's unexpected death, sinking bonelessly into a handy chair, a handkerchief clutched in one hand the only sign of emotion. Having absorbed the shock but giving no hint of her true feelings (grief something that

115

belonged behind closed doors) she sees herself as rising magnificently to the occasion, drawing on reserves of confidence and courage unsuspected by any of her friends . . . or indeed by her dead husband. Then, the funeral over (hers a lone figure following the coffin) she takes charge of her life, selling the house and moving into a flat, buying scarves and going to the theatre, life suddenly sunlit, roomy and accommodating.

Upstairs . . . and on the few occasions he wasn't round at his daughter-in-law's . . . Mr Forbes is finding release in scribbling notes on a saga of torture and rape in Renaissance Italy which he plans to work up on the internet for the benefit of another unseemly friend he has found for himself in Paterson, New Jersey.

People would have said this was a happy marriage, which it sort of was.

Mrs Forbes poured herself another sherry.

* * *

Having just completed a tour of the bank's east of England mortgages ripe for repossession Graham was driving through Peterborough when his phone rang.

'Hi, Toby. It's Gary. Where are you?'

'Peterborough.'

'Peterborough! Some people have all the luck. Having a good time?'

'No,' said Graham shortly.

'Why? It says here it has a Norman cathedral.'

Not being an imminent mortgage risk the cathedral had not figured in Graham's itinerary. 'How's the lady wife?'

116

'I can't hear,' said Graham. 'You're breaking up,' and he put the phone down.

Somewhere around Newark it rang again.

'Where are you?'

'About fifty miles north of where I was before and I'm not sure I like this.'

'Like what?'

'You calling me all the time.'

'All the time? Twice by my calculation. You should be flattered.'

'Why?' said Graham. 'I pay, remember.'

'That is crude. That is unworthy of you, Toby. A person has feelings.'

'Anyway,' said Graham 'I can't today. I don't have any cash on me.'

'We could make it a freebie.'

Careful about money an offer like this would normally have appealed to Graham but even he could see that acceptance risked turning what was a transaction into a relationship.

'No. I've just found some in another pocket. Where shall I meet you?'

It was dark by the time Graham pulled alongside the waiting Gary in an empty car park, Kevin giving Toby a brief hug before walking him to the side door of a dark, oldish building where he punched in a code and let himself in.

'Where are you taking me?' said Graham as they walked down a bleak corridor lined with identical doors. It seemed to be some sort of hostel, the room Gary let them into furnished with the bare essentials . . . bed, washbasin, locker and with no evidence that it was occupied even by Gary. It was suffocatingly hot.

'You've come down in the world,' said Graham.

117

'This?' said Kevin mildly as he took his trousers off. 'No. It's the workplace.'

'And what were the other places. The luxury apartment. The house in Roundhay?'

'They were the workplace too.'

'What do you do?' said Graham.

'I told you. I'm a panel beater.'

Putting his shoes neatly by the side of the bed Graham noted the dust and fluff on the floor. 'Aren't you going to lock the door?' said Graham.

'What for? There's nobody else here.'

Some clients might have been turned on by the institutional nature of the surroundings but not Graham.

'Where are we?' he said.

'I've told you. Work. Take your shirt off.'

Reflecting that he was the one who was supposed to be calling the tune Graham nevertheless took it off and his pants too. Unsurprisingly it was a less satisfactory session than they had had in the past, at one point even getting acrimonious when Graham drew the line, and quite early on in the proceedings Graham resolved that however keen Gary was this wasn't going to happen again.

Gary was leaning on his elbow while Graham lay on his back.

'What are you thinking about?' said Kevin.

Graham was actually thinking how much, other things being equal, he preferred his safe, cosy marital bed but he had the sense not to say so. He was also wondering how long it had to be before he could decently take his leave. Though before that there was the question of payment.

'How's married life?'

'Fine.'

'How's the bank?'

'The bank is fine.'

Kevin considered.

'Tell me. Does your mother know you're gay?'

'I'm married. That's all she knows.'

Graham reached for his shirt and started to put his clothes on though Kevin seemed in no hurry to do the same.

'They're always supposed to know, mothers.'

'You don't know mine.'

'True,' said Kevin, 'but what if she were to find out?'

'How would she do that? How much do I owe you? Same as last time?'

'How much do you love your mother?'

Graham stood, money in hand.

'What sort of a question is that? How much do you love your mother?'

'My mother knows.'

Graham had had enough of this.

'Same as before then?' and he put down some notes.

Kevin looked at them distastefully.

'Oh, I think we should say more than that. This is your mother, after all.'

'Oh no,' said Graham. 'Oh no,' and he picked up the money and put it back in his wallet.

'I'm not having truck with any of that. Any of that and I'll go straight to the police.'

'Very sensible,' said Kevin, hands clasped behind his head. 'And you wouldn't have far to go. I am the police. Now, take your clothes off and before we talk business perhaps we could reconsider the proposal I made you earlier.'

Graham had meant it when he had said he would

go to the police and an hour later when he had made his escape he considered going straightaway. He then thought he should sleep on it and ideally talk it over with Betty. Sensible though this was it was obviously out of the question and in the event a week or two passed before, steeling himself for the inevitable embarrassment, he took steps to report the culprit.

The police station was unexpectedly civilised, tubs of geraniums on the doorstep with automatic doors sliding open on a bland reception area, a print by Van Gogh on one wall and one by Lowry on another, the ambience saying more about customer satisfaction than it did about law enforcement.

The desk sergeant, a kindly looking figure with white hair, was already dealing with a woman at the counter.

'I'm just seeing to this client but I shan't be a moment.' He indicated the reception area. 'Take a seat. There's coffee on the go though you've just missed the croissants.'

He turned back to the woman.

'Now what was he like?'

'Who?'

'The gentleman who assaulted you. Did you notice if he was black at all?'

The reassuring atmosphere notwithstanding Graham was still nervous and went in search of the loo.

This, too, turned out to be surprisingly upmarket with distant music that Betty though not Graham would have been able to identify as *The Lark Ascending*.

Then someone had been thoughtful enough

to position a bowl of potpourri on the window sill, another touch which, had Graham not been preoccupied, would surely have got a tick.

As he came out the desk sergeant was just finishing with his customer while a woman PC waited to take charge.

'And shall I put you down for counselling?'

'What do you think?'

'It's good to talk,' said PC Valerie and took her off down the corridor.

'We can't always solve the crime,' said the sergeant, 'but at least we can make it easier to bear. Now, sir. Sorry to have kept you waiting. How can we help?'

Graham had decided to come straight to the point.

'The thing is,' and he leaned confidentially over the counter, 'it's a bit difficult. While I'm not exactly gay and am in fact happily married I've got myself into a bit of a fix and I'm being blackmailed.'

'Dear me,' said the desk sergeant. 'There's no need for that in this day and age. Blackmail! We aren't living in the 1950s. Well, you're in luck. I happen to know our community liaison officer is on the premises and you can have a little chat with him. I shan't keep you a moment.' And he went off down the corridor saying, 'Blackmail! Dear oh dear.'

Heartened by his sympathetic reception and relieved at the prospect of sharing his troubles Graham resumed his seat in the reception area where he idly leafed through some of the literature scattered about the low table. Turning a page of the local bulletin he came upon a photograph of a young policeman, looking shy but fetching in his

uniform as he was being presented with an award for services to the community. It was Gary.

Not having kept abreast of liberation and its advancements Graham was slightly startled to find the award had been given to Gary (whose name appeared to be Kevin) for services to the community and in particular in his capacity as gay liaison officer. Having come out himself, 'as a policeman, an act of great personal courage', Kevin/Gary had been giving talks in schools, churches and to community groups, and was thought to be personally responsible for a significant fall in hate crime in the neighbourhood.

He was about to read on when somewhere down the corridor a door opened and Graham heard the sound of voices. Not daring to look back or to check who it was Graham ran down the steps, waiting an agonised second or two before the doors slid open and he could flee the premises.

* * *

It is a few days later and Betty is dawdling over her computer.

'Did you ever wonder,' she said, 'whether Graham might be gay?'

Mr Forbes senior put on his glasses and considered.

'It had occurred to me,' he said, 'only then he married you so I assumed I must be mistaken.'

It was the afternoon and they were in bed.

'What about you?'

'It worried me,' said Betty 'that he spent so much time on his fingernails, although men do moisturise nowadays, don't they?'

'They do,' agreed Mr Forbes (who didn't). 'He was always fastidious even as a boy and he had an umbrella at a very early age. Still, I wouldn't worry about it. He likes you, that's the main thing.'

'Yes,' said Betty, 'but he is gay. I've known for a while.' (She'd followed up some of the websites he'd been visiting.) 'I was just bothered that you didn't.'

'Is it a problem?' said his father.

'Not as such,' said Betty. 'And he does very well.'

'Which just leaves Muriel,' said Mr Forbes. 'There'd be a problem there.'

'Has she made any progress on the computer?'

'What do you think?' said Mr Forbes.

Betty frowned, her fingers scampering over the keys.

'What's the matter?'

Betty shook her head as she brought Graham's personal account up on the screen. 'I can't work it out. He's been making some very odd payments.'

Though Graham and (as he was still bound to call him) Gary now met regularly Graham never mentioned his visit to the police station or that he knew of Kevin's respected position in the community . . . a role which even Graham could see rendered him as vulnerable to blackmail as his victim. How, though, could he turn the tables? Short of coming out and telling Betty and his mother for the moment there was nothing to be done.

A casualty of the heightened commerciality of the relationship between the two men was any pleasure Graham might have been expected to glean from their connection. He did what he was told glumly and with no joy, never able to forget

123

that he was being physically humiliated and was paying for the privilege besides with, most injured, his pride.

His marked lack of enthusiasm, while entirely understandable, still managed to irk his tormentor who felt that some minimal rapture was owing. But it was not forthcoming and Graham was not a good enough actor to simulate it.

'The spoilsport,' thought Kevin. Still, and he trousered another grand, there were compensations.

In time, though, boredom took its toll even on Kevin and more and more when they met money changed hands but nothing else.

The hangover from these unwilling trysts affected Betty, too. The exuberance that had made Graham such an enlivening partner was now virtually extinguished. He came to bed and went to sleep, but often now she would wake in the night and find him awake too.

At first Betty thought this was what was to be expected, the shine going off the marriage as it was supposed to do. But there were other more disturbing developments. Undressing, Graham had always put his clothes neatly on or over the back of the chair, his shoes, socks inside, tucked cosily under the bed. This new Graham now left his shirt on the floor and his shoes all over the place so that Betty wondered at first if he was having a breakdown before deciding he wasn't imaginative enough for that.

Something was wrong, though, and his fingernails were a disgrace.

Chaste as their life together had become, it was not wanting in affection. Indeed since Graham's

trouble he had become a far kinder and more considerate and appealing person than he had ever been before. He came to his wife for comfort and reassurance though over what he was never specific. 'Life' was the nearest he got to it.

'Is it work?' Betty asked.

'Not really.'

'You're not ill?'

He shook his head mutely.

'You're so good to me,' he would mumble before drifting off to troubled sleep. Tonight, though, he lay awake and talked about their future, saying he didn't want to spend the rest of his life in a bank and had she ever thought of Australia.

Betty had never thought of Australia, being quite happy with Alwoodley. So she was about to 'talk it through' as he put it when Graham leaped out of bed and peered through the curtains.

'What is it?'

'Nothing,' said Graham. 'I thought there was a car outside.'

*　　　*　　　*

'At first,' said Betty, 'I thought he was just stealing from the bank, only why I couldn't think as there's always plenty of money in his account.'

They were in bed again, the laptop eponymously open on her lap, Mr Forbes reading.

She didn't say this to Mr Forbes but what shocked Betty wasn't the peculation itself; it was that the amounts involved, while not trivial, were relatively small. Acquisitive though Graham was and bold though he thought himself he had always been modest in his aspirations and limited in

125

his ambitions, how limited he himself had never appreciated. He had never realised, for instance, that what he took to be Betty's fortune was actually only the accumulated interest from her real fortune which lay elsewhere. In the light of this the amounts that Graham was embezzling from the bank were negligible, but they would need to be repaid and repaid quickly before an audit showed them up.

Actually she was doing Graham an injustice. He was modest in his assumptions, it's true, but so, too, was Kevin and it was his demands that dictated the withdrawals, each as limited in his expectations as the other.

'So where is the money going?' said Mr Forbes.

'Give me five minutes,' said Betty.

Simpler, of course, would have been to ask the man himself, 'Are you being blackmailed?' but several considerations made this course of action unfeasible. For a start it blew Betty's cover as the simple but adoring wife, knowing nothing of money or accounts or the world in general. Bad enough that she would have to reveal that she had been poring over his bank statements and in the process had sufficient know-how to spot payments that were dubious or inexplicable; but more generally undesirable in Betty's view would be the transformation of their relationship that must come about were Graham to realise she knew that he was gay (if even occasionally). Lacking in intellectual stimulation though it was, their set-up seemed to Betty pretty well satisfactory. The adjustments consequent on either of them coming clean were too radical (and too tedious) even to contemplate . . . his bluster, her forbearance, no: cards on tables was not a solution. 'I've found him,' said Betty . . .

126

<p style="text-align:center">* * *</p>

Graham's mother was just thinking of having an early sherry when the doorbell went. It was a policeman.

'Good afternoon, Mrs Forbes. I am the Crime Prevention Officer. There has been a spate of burglaries in the neighbourhood and we're conducting a survey of home security.'

He showed her an identity card.

'May I come in?'

'Of course.'

But then he didn't, just waiting on the doorstep.

'No offence, Mrs Forbes, but you have already made two mistakes. One, you opened the door straightaway without putting it on the chain before ascertaining who the caller might be. Two, you didn't even look at my identification. Check it out.'

He showed it to her again and she looked more carefully. It was a card for a swimming club, the policeman . . . if he was a policeman . . . half-naked in swimming trunks.

'It's a lovely photo,' said Mrs Forbes, 'but it's not the legal one.'

'Quite so,' said the Crime Prevention Officer. 'You sometimes have to commit crimes in order to prevent them. This is the one you should have been shown,' and he handed her another card with a (clothed this time) photograph and which attested to his status as Crime Prevention Officer.

'Now, Mrs Forbes, having established my credentials, may I come in?'

'Certainly,' said Mrs Forbes. 'I was just going to have some tea.'

* * *

'He could have been anybody,' said Mr Forbes later.

'Yes. He told me that, only I know a policeman when I see one. And if you're so concerned for my well-being you should try being at home more often. How long does it take to put up a shelf?'

'The shelves are finished, I'm doing the draught excluders now.'

* * *

'What did he look like?' said Graham.

'Very handsome,' said his mother. 'He showed me a picture of him in swimming trunks.'

'The policeman? What on earth for?'

'To test me. Then he showed me the proper one with his clothes on. He's the Crime Prevention Officer.'

'So you keep saying. What did you tell him?'

'I didn't have to tell him anything. He knew it all. It's on the internet, apparently.'

'The internet?'

'The computer. One of those things.'

'What you don't realise,' said Graham, 'is that now I'm higher up in the bank we're all much more vulnerable. Bankers' families get kidnapped on a regular basis as a way of getting into the safe.'

'Not in Alwoodley, surely. I said to him, I don't like the police knowing all our details and he said it was just to be on the safe side. Though he had one or two things wrong. He thought your name was Toby. I said, "Toby?" I said you'd once had a dog called Toby when you were little, do you

remember? that smelly little article that we had to get rid of . . . that was the only Toby I knew. We laughed.'

* * *

'Nice woman your mother,' said Kevin. 'Adores you.'

'Yes,' said Graham. 'That's the only reason I'm here.'

It was another bleak car park.

'Shame you got married, though. She wasn't expecting that.'

'Leave her alone.'

'I beg your pardon.'

'What's my mother got to do with you? I'm paying, aren't I? Leave her alone.'

'I have to do my duty. The premises are inadequately protected. They don't even have an alarm bell.'

* * *

So in due course Mrs Forbes senior's policeman made what he called 'a follow-up visit', bringing the homeowner the latest literature on laser technology in the service of crime prevention. She had poured him a sherry and they were in the lounge discussing where, should she invest in some sensors, they could best be positioned. His standing on a chair to point out the preferred locations gave Mrs Forbes a chance to admire the same well-muscled back that her son had had occasion to stroke the fateful night before his wedding. Now, though, it was filling out a crisp white uniform shirt, set off by epaulettes, a

pager thrust into the back pocket.

'And all this advice is free?' said Mrs Forbes.

'Absolutely, because from the police point of view, it pays for itself. The more secure the premises the fewer the break-ins.

'Mrs Forbes,' said the policeman.

'Please,' said Mrs Forbes, 'call me Muriel . . .' And she put her hand on his knee.

When an hour or so later Mr Forbes let himself in it was to find the householder and the Crime Prevention Officer both on the sofa where she was showing him the photograph albums with pictures of Graham as a boy.

'That's Toby,' she said pointing to a scruffy Scotty cradled in the boy's arms. 'Dreadful dog. Always rolling in things.'

*　　　*　　　*

'Does he know Graham?' said Mr Forbes after the policeman had gone.

'Know him?' said Mrs Forbes. 'Why should he? He's a policeman.'

*　　　*　　　*

Having had a good look round a different car park, this one multi-storey, Kevin kept it under surveillance for at least an hour before suddenly slipping into the passenger seat beside Betty.

'How can I help you?'

'I'm Graham's wife.'

'Is that why you're crying? Though I have to say I don't know any Grahams. Do you mean Toby?'

'Possibly.' Betty blew her nose.

'If his name is Graham why does he call himself Toby?'

'How much do you want?' said Betty. 'I mean, to call it a day?'

Ten minutes later their talk satisfactorily concluded Kevin got out of the car.

On the other side of the car park Mr Forbes took another photograph and switched off his recording machine.

'Nice doing business with you,' said Kevin. Which is not what he said when a copy of the CD came through the letter box next morning.

'We do lead an exciting life,' said Mr Forbes as they drove home. 'It never used to be like this.' So now the phone calls abruptly and inexplicably ceased and with no word from his sometime tormentor Graham's marital vigour reasserted itself and, his fingernails once more immaculate, life returned to its old ways. It puzzled Graham that there was no comeback at the bank and when he eventually came to look into it he could find no trace in the accounts that anything had ever been wrong. When something bothered him at work he would normally talk it over with Betty, which in this case he couldn't do so for a while he remained uneasy, eventually deciding that Kevin being a policeman this had led him . . . or the force possibly . . . to make the necessary reimbursement just for safety's sake.

* * *

Mrs Forbes, the unwitting beneficiary of the thwarted blackmail, remains unwitting, ignorant both of the peculations of her son and the ingenuity

131

of her daughter-in-law who, along with her husband, were concerned only to safeguard her innocence.

Such concern might be thought of as wholly admirable except that self-servingness comes into it, too, and a distaste for disturbance and the attachment of all these parties to a landscape that is familiar and which the convulsive revelation of her son's sexuality would certainly reshape.

There was, too . . . and this may be harder to understand . . . there was affection. Monstrous as she was, a tyrant and a snob, Graham's mother was an ogre of such long-standing that her feelings (though they could often only be guessed at) nevertheless merited respect. Not yet an ancient monument she was a survival and on that score alone her outlook and her armour-plated ignorance merited preservation.

None of this would have found much sympathy with the lady in question, the object of these elaborate precautions almost certainly viewing such consideration as neither necessary nor appropriate. Graham's mother did not need shielding from the knowledge that her beloved son was homosexual: she had known it all along. It was an opinion she had never bothered to share with her husband but before Betty had come into their lives she had always thought Graham 'not the marrying sort' and it was one of her (unspoken) grievances against Betty that the marriage had made it necessary for her to revise that opinion.

So when Kevin, in a last shot of his bolt (and more out of pique than self-interest), came round one afternoon and spilled the (long-postponed) beans Mrs Forbes was relieved rather than surprised: it was a return to the natural order of

things. She had been right all along. True she put on a good amateur performance of what she imagined a devastated mother's reaction might be, staring hard and grim-jawed out of the window as she contemplated the wreck of all her hopes, a performance so convincing it impelled Kevin to lay a consoling hand on her shoulder.

This was a mistake.

She poured them both a sherry. Looking at this delightful young man she could hardly blame her son who had, after all, impeccable taste. Marriage to someone as unprepossessing as Betty had been a lapse, which, thankfully, had only been temporary, the implication being that what a man needed in a woman (and which Mrs Forbes saw herself as providing) was perfection: given anything less a chap such as Graham was not to be blamed if he washed his hands of the whole gender and shopped elsewhere.

'Can you blame him?' she said to the captive Kevin. 'It takes a woman to understand.'

Carried to its logical conclusion, of course, this free-market theory of sexual preference is hardly tenable as it would see the ranks of deviance swollen by droves of disappointed normality. Not that Mrs Forbes cares about that, her thoughts for the moment busy with a more immediate breach of suburban rectitude.

In conclusion, how much better . . . how much *healthier* . . . had all these persons, these family members, been more candid with one another right from the start.

As it is there's every chance Betty will grow bored with Graham, with divorce the obvious solution. Except that they now have twins, whom

they both adore, and besides divorce might mean that some awkward truths would have to be told and neither of them wants that.

That Mr Forbes still from time to time sleeps with his daughter-in-law and leads a vigorous fantasy life on the internet besides would shame both his wife and his son did it ever come to light; but why should it, the only clue to their clandestine relationship Betty's disproportionate grief on Mr Forbes's death from a heart attack a few years later? The death of her husband while at last giving Mrs Forbes occasion to play for real her often-rehearsed scene of sudden bereavement also draws Graham and his mother closer together, much as they had been before his marriage. Then, having had one sherry too many and thinking the better to bond with her boy and to show him she's still in the game, Mrs Forbes comes clean on her escapade with Kevin. It had been more short-lived than she let on, their brief relationship curtailed when, a few months later, Kevin perished in a high-speed motorway car chase, a death that might seem to have more to do with narrative tidiness than any driving without due care and attention. Far from drawing him closer to his mother the revelation of this liaison, however perfunctory, shocks and embarrasses Graham, who feels that his mother might have had the consideration to keep this distasteful news to herself. It also abuts far too closely on his own sexual preferences, still, he fondly imagines, a secret known only to himself.

Graham goes home and tells Betty about Mrs Forbes and her fling with Kevin, 'this gay policeman' as Graham describes him. Betty, who, unsurprisingly, is unsurprised, promises never to

tell a soul, the souls she particularly must not tell the twins. She also mustn't tell them what Graham still hasn't told her, namely that their father is not as other men are and likely to go on being so. Though if he'd told her that in the first place he would never have married her and there would be no story.

But the most secret secret of all which Betty alone knows is that the father of the twins is probably their grandfather.

So the secrets abound, with Betty more richly endowed with them as she is with everything else. Still, for all that everybody, while not happy, is not unhappy about it. And so they go on.